VALENTINE FOR DANTE

VALENTINE FOR DANTE

QUEENS & KNIGHTS BOOK 3

M KAY NOIR

Valentine for Dante (Second Edition)

Copyright @ M Kay Noir 2024

Valentine for Dante, First edition 2024

Cover Design @ Lerusha Reddy

All rights reserved.

For those who crave the freedom to explore desire without the confines of labels and pre-assigned boxes

CONTENTS

A WORD OF CAUTION

This book is intended for a mature audience only. It contains often graphic scenes between consenting adults.

Refer to mkaynoir.com/dante for the full TW/CW list (on-page and off-page mentions).

If at any point this book makes you feel unsafe, please take a break and consider whether you want to continue.

Mental health matters.

BOOK PLAYLIST

Listen on Spotify or navigate via mkaynoir.com/dante

1. The Heavy, *Short Change Hero*

2. Chvrches & Robert Smith, *How Not to Drown*

3. Muse, *Time is Running Out*

4. Bad Omens, *The Death of Peace of Mind*

5. Nothing but Thieves, *If I Were You*

6. Editors, *Sugar*

7. Queens of the Stone Age, *No One Knows*

8. The Kills, *Let It Drop*

9. Chevelle, *The Meddler*

10. Puscifer, *The Arsonist*

11. Jack White, *Love is Blindness*

12. Nataly Dawn, *Careless Whisper*

13. Måneskin, *Valentine*

14. Florence & the Machine, *What Kind of Man*

15. Jamie T, *Don't you Find*

16. Asaf Avidan, *Different Pulses*

17. The Black Keys, *Weight of Love*

18. Stone Sour, *Wicked Game*

19. Magnolia Electric Co. & Jason Molina, *Almost Was Good Enough*

CHAPTER ONE

SURPRISE

DANTE...

T he neon skyline burns into my retinas like an old scar reopening. Twenty-five years, and still my body remembers—every muscle locking up, throat closing, heart hammering against my ribs like it's trying to escape. *Vegas.* The city I swore I'd never see again.

"Surprise, darling!" Danica's voice bubbles with excitement, a sharp contrast to the ice spreading through my veins.

Her hand finds my arm, trying to pull me up, but I'm frozen in place. The leather seat creaks under my white-knuckled grip.

Through the plane's window, Las Vegas sprawls across the desert like a beautiful poison, all glitter and danger and memories I've spent decades trying to bury.

I shouldn't be here. Not after what happened.

1

"What's wrong?" Danica's smile falters as she reads my face. My Queen, so proud of her Valentine's surprise, watching it crumble.

"It's nothing." The lie tastes bitter.

"I've booked us an entire weekend of surprises..." Her enthusiasm dims with each word, like Vegas lights at dawn.

My jaw clenches involuntarily. "I wish you didn't."

The cabin suddenly feels like a trap, walls closing in. Every breath comes shorter than the last. Twenty-five years, but I can still hear those final words, still feel the weight of that night pressing against my chest. The memory makes my lungs seize.

"Aren't you surprised?"

Surprised? I'm drowning in fragments of the past—the incessant shouting, the blood on marble, promises turned to ash. The runway lights blur through the window, then and now bleeding together until I can't tell which is which.

"We need to go back—now." My voice shakes despite my efforts to steady it.

As much as I hate displeasing my Domme, this is bigger than any of us. After what happened with the Riccis, I vowed to protect Danica at all costs, but I can't protect her here, not in Vegas.

"What do you mean *back*?"

"We can't be here; we must leave immediately." The words tumble out, barely coherent through the roar in my head.

"Why?" she asks and the unanswerable echoes through my mind. *Why? Why? WHY?*

"Dante?" Danica's lip catches between her teeth—a nervous tell that usually melts me. Not now.

"Tell the pilot we're turning around." My fists clench until I feel nails break skin. The pain helps, gives me something to focus on besides panic.

"You're being weird, Dante. I thought you'd be happy to get away?"

How do I explain? How do I tell her about what happened back then?

"It's dangerous, Danica. We need to leave immediately." It's not untrue.

The seatbelt clicks open like a gunshot. My joints protest as I unfold myself—too tall for this luxury cage, too old for these ghosts.

At the back of the plane, Emilio sits silent, watchful. He was there that day, saw everything. We've never spoken of it—some regrets are too heavy for words.

"Surely we can stay the night at least?" Danica is not letting up.

I shoulder past her, gentle but firm. Can't look at her face, can't see the hurt I'm causing. Later. I'll explain later, when we're safe, when we're far from this city of broken promises and beautiful lies.

"Let me speak to the pilot."

"Dante!"

But I'm already moving, driven by pure survival instinct. Get out. Get her out. Before the past catches up.

The pilot startles when I burst into the cockpit, her brown eyes flashing with annoyance. She's young, probably early thirties, her uniform crisp and professional—exactly the type to follow every rule to the letter.

"Can I help you, sir?" Her politeness is razor-thin. She doesn't know who I am. Doesn't know what this city means to me.

"Get everything ready for our return. There has been a mistake." My voice sounds strange in my own ears, tight with barely controlled anxiety.

"Not possible, unfortunately." She shrugs, dismissive in a way no one has dared be with me in years. If she were on my payroll, this would be her last flight. But she isn't.

Rage bubbles under my skin, hot and familiar. "We must return at once."

"Even if I felt like doing another four hours without rest—which, I might add, is dangerous—we can't." She doesn't even look up from her instruments.

"Can't or won't?" The words come out like a growl.

"I said *can't*, didn't I? Air traffic control restrictions. This is a high-traffic area. We're not cleared for take-off today." Her matter-of-fact tone makes my teeth grind.

The co-pilot shrinks under my glare, but he's not the one I need to convince.

"Then get us cleared. Money is no problem." My voice trembles, betraying the edge of desperation I'm trying to hide.

Her eyes narrow. "We're in Vegas...*sir*. There's money all over. Get in line. We cannot leave without clearance." The pause before "sir" is deliberately insulting.

I'm about to show her exactly who she's dealing with when small fingers wrap around my arm, pulling me back. Danica's touch anchors me, her hand lifting my chin until I'm forced to meet her gaze.

"Stop harassing the crew, Dante. You're being unnecessary. Let's just get off this plane and check in."

"We could've gone anywhere. *Anywhere* else." The words come out more plea than protest.

"You know I've always wanted to see Vegas."

"It's dangerous here." The understatement of the century.

"Danger comes with your job. Everywhere is dangerous with you. That's why we have Emilio to protect us."

I open my mouth but close it again. There's no argument that will get us out of this glittering trap tonight. *Cazzo!*

My eyes drift to the windows again. Twenty-five years, but the city still pulses with the same seductive danger. Different buildings, same secrets. Different players, same game.

"Dante, we'll be fine. I made the booking under a fake name, don't worry. We can be discreet," she tries to reassure me.

I look to Emilio for backup, but my old guard just shakes his head. Even he knows better than to challenge Danica's determination.

"Why did you agree to this, Emilio? You know..." *You know what happened here. You know what it cost me.*

"I apologize, boss. I didn't know she was taking us here." His face remains carefully neutral, decades of practice at hiding what he knows.

"Don't blame Emilio. I just told him we're going on holiday and he needs to come. The blinds stayed shut the whole trip—I wanted it to be a surprise." Danica's lower lip trembles. "I thought you would be happy."

The hurt in her voice breaks something in me. I pull her close, wrapping her small frame in my arms. "I'm sorry, *Tesoro*. I know you put in so much effort."

"You always have so many secrets." She sighs against my chest. "I thought you'd told me everything."

"Some secrets I hide even from myself," I murmur into her hair, knowing she wants more, knowing I can't give it. Not yet. Maybe not ever.

"I'm sorry," I whisper again, pressing a kiss to her crown.

She melts against me. "It's okay. I know you'll tell me when you're ready."

When she rises on tiptoes to kiss me, I let myself drown in her—the familiar scent of her skin, the taste of her mouth, the solid reality of her in my arms. For a moment, the panic recedes.

I cup her face in my hands, studying those wild eyes I love so much. "We'll keep a low profile and head out as soon as we can, understood?"

Her smile turns mischievous at the corners. "Yes, Don Fera. Are you done giving orders now...*boy*?" Danica asks, a playful yet stern look crossing her face.

A "boy" at the ripe old age of 44? *Yes, Ma'am*. Only for Danica.

With a single word, every changes; Danica regains her power. She reaches up, unbuttons the top button of my shirt, and assertively tugs me down to her eye level, finger hooked through the metal loop in my hidden leather collar that only she knows about.

Gasping for air as the collar chokes me, I hunch down to my owner, staring into her eyes until my breathing returns to its normal pace. Balance has been restored.

"I'm sorry, *Miss*," I whisper the last word. I know Emilio knows about Danica and my dynamic, he must know, but I know my secrets are safe with him—like what happened in Vegas more than two decades ago.

"I don't like your tone. I think it's time we changed it, don't you?" Danica whispers, her face inches from mine.

I nod submissively, ready to give her everything—even Vegas. Just for tonight.

Danica grins triumphantly, kissing my cheek before uttering the two words that we both know are my entire undoing: "Good boy."

I groan loudly, the power of her soft-spoken words unmistakable.

Before I can change my mind, Danica buttons up my shirt again and takes my hand, leading me to the exit.

The warm desert air hits me as soon as we disembark from the air-conditioned cocoon but it can't stop the involuntary shiver that runs down my spine.

This is a bad idea.

CHAPTER TWO

DEJECTED

DANICA...

E ven in the harsh light of the desert sun, I am mesmerized by the array of colors flashing past my window in the short drive from the airport to our hotel. The city of sin looks even more spectacular than in the movies! *How is this place even real?*

For a moment, I even forget about Dante's brooding, fully distracted by the shiny scenery.

My glum knight doesn't say much during the drive; he just stares out the window restlessly, those emerald eyes darting around like he's expecting something I'm not expecting.

I wish I knew what was going on. Sure, he says it's "dangerous" here but I've seen Dante in the face of danger—he doesn't even flinch. This is something else. I find myself studying his face intently for any trace of an answer but I am met with an impenetrable stone wall.

At least it's a good-looking stone wall. Handsome even on a bad day, nobody would ever say Dante is almost two decades older than me. His on-staff barber somehow manages to consistently achieve the perfect fade, skillfully taming those unruly dark curly locks and leaving his thick beard meticulously trimmed, accentuating that prominent jawline I love to shower in kisses.

Pity about that jaw currently being clenched in tension. Dante is clearly not happy to be here. This is not how I thought this weekend would play out. Not at all.

I've been so excited over the past month, sneakily planning the getaway, hiding it all from Dante. I'd imagined his response countless times, how surprised he'd be to find himself whisked away on a special Valentine's outing to Vegas. He'd be so grateful for the escape from work, I thought. We'd fuck on every surface and paint the town red, spending more money than was sensible and then some. That was the dream!

My dream only—not Dante's—I now realize. *Where did I go so wrong?* We've been together for more than a year now; I thought I knew him. Sure, sometimes he'd complain and pretend he didn't want to go somewhere, but he always gave in to me eventually.

This time is different. This time I've apparently fucked up. But I still don't know how.

The disappointment weighs heavy on me as I stare at my hands like I'm trying to see through them. I wish I could run away to sulk without an audience. But we are stuck together in Vegas—at least for a day or two.

An unexpected soft thud breaks the silence, a jolt that yanks me back to the present. The impact reverberates through the car, a sickening vibration that unsettles my stomach.

The driver curses under his breath and yanks the wheel to the left, but it's too late.

"What was that?" I ask quickly, jerking my head around, alarmed.

"Just a dog," the driver replies nonchalantly, picking up speed without so much as a second glance.

"Is it dead?" I squint, but I see nothing out the back window—just dust.

The driver seemingly couldn't care less. "Probably just wounded," he dismisses me.

"Go back," I request between gritted teeth.

"Danica—" Dante starts, but I cut him off. Trembling, I raise my voice, pulling the vehicle to an immediate stop. "I said, *go back*!"

The driver looks around at Dante for direction, but the tattooed god just shrugs. We both know who calls the shots, even if the driver doesn't.

"Yes, Ma'am," the driver concedes. Reluctantly, he puts on the car's hazard lights and reverses to where the bundle of black-and-white fur lies discarded in the dust.

As tempted as I am to give the guy an earful about calling me Ma'am, my priority right now is the dog.

Emilio and Dante exchange knowing looks, but neither says anything. They don't try to stop me when I jump out, cars whizzing past me loudly, or when I hunch down next to the whining pup in the dirt.

It's still alive but its leg seems crushed. My heart melts as the little creature looks at me with big eyes. It looks like a Border Collie mix of some sort, a mutt for sure. It's still small but, judging by the state of its rugged coat, it's used to living rough.

I take off my expensive faux leather jacket and wrap it around the dog, carefully picking it up. It whimpers meekly when I hug it to my body protectively but doesn't try to escape. *Poor thing.*

"We need to get it to a vet," I tell the driver as I slide back into my seat, the wounded canine on my lap.

"It is just a dirty mongrel. Leave it," the cocky driver snarks.

Dante moves so quickly that the asshole doesn't see him coming until it's too late; until Dante's thick arm is folded around his neck, pressing against his windpipe forcefully. "She *said* take us to the vet. It is in your best interest to give Miss Matthews what she wants, are we clear?" Dante's voice is loud and assertive—it's the one he uses when people owe him money or someone's about to lose a finger.

The driver nods profusely, his eyes betraying his fear. "Yes, sir. Sorry, sir."

"Good. Now drive!" Dante lets go, and the man gasps for air, trying to fill his lungs again.

Without another word, the prick puts his foot back on the accelerator as Dante sits back in his seat, a deep scowl etched on his face.

"Thank you." I smile faintly at my Don, still holding the wounded hound close.

"You'll probably have to throw that jacket away." Dante's face softens as he leans over to get a closer look at the rescue.

"I don't care about the jacket," I reply, holding the puppy like a baby, sheltering it from further harm.

"Danica, I—" Dante starts, his voice slow, heavy.

"It's okay, baby. We can talk at the hotel." Reaching over with my free hand, I squeeze his fingers in mine.

He nods solemnly and gets back to his brooding, watching the lights fly by as we get swallowed up by the hustle and bustle of the city.

This is my first time in Vegas. I'd always wanted to go, but my family never had that kind of money. Plus, it's super far away if you don't have access to a fancy private plane like Dante does.

Growing up, all I had were books filled with extraordinary adventures set against lavish casino backdrops and movies where people drank expensive cocktails in tiny glasses—I wanted to see it all for myself.

But I wasn't looking now, my full attention was locked on the warm body in my lap, stroking it gently behind the ears. *Please don't die,* I plead silently.

Luckily, the vet isn't far away. We reach it within minutes. A friendly nurse with a tight ponytail assures me that the dog is in good hands and that they'll look after it. I leave the credit card details, Dante's, and saunter back to the car, where the men are waiting in silence.

The hotel I booked is only a few minutes away, and the driver is as relieved to get rid of us as I am to get rid of him. As he unloads our bags, I make a mental note to never use that service again. *Asshole.*

We check in without any other eventful happenings—Mister and Missus Caruso for the penthouse suite, please, and thank you. I'd Googled a list of Italian surnames and that one seemed cute. I could see myself being Missus Danica Caruso, wife of Dante Caruso. *Imagine that?*

Emilio gets his own suite one floor down from us, complete with an extravagant view and a jacuzzi I know he probably won't use. But I want to spoil him for everything he does for us. The old guard doesn't see the point but accepts his keycard, nonetheless.

Our own suite is even fancier but I hardly feel like celebrating our arrival. Everything feels so...anticlimactic.

Dante lets out a loaded sigh when the door finally closes behind us, the private elevator disappearing down the 47 floors again and leaving us at the top. He seems relieved. Why, I still do not know. The question will drive me mad!

Trying to force my mind away from it, I focus on my surroundings instead, trying to regain some of the excitement I'd lost since opening the plane's blinds, shouting "Surprise!" at a rather unimpressed partner.

Our hotel suite is next-level lavish, straight out of a *White Lotus* episode. Rich hues and gleaming surfaces greet me as I explore the large space, a stylish retreat high above the city's chaotic pulse. It cost more than my entire year's salary when I still worked at the restaurant, but I don't even flinch at spending that kind of money anymore. If Dante doesn't care, why should I?

The first thing that strikes me is the view: floor-to-ceiling windows frame the magical Las Vegas skyline like a living masterpiece. It's way more impressive than anything else in the room. The shiny-as-fuck crystal chandelier takes up way too much space, if you ask me.

My ex once promised he would take me to Vegas. It was back in our happy years, before I found out about all the cheating and the betrayal. But just like so many times before (and after): it was all just a tall tale, a lie, to try and keep me trapped in our unhappy world. He never got me the presents he said he would either, or the Valentine's surprise I longed for year after year. Spoils were meant for others, but not for me—clearly.

I return from my improvised tour of the space to find Dante pouring himself a stiff whiskey. He seems a bit more relaxed now. Still, he feels so far away, like a stranger.

Fixing myself a drink too, I take a seat near the window, stretching out on a lavish white settee I would never buy for myself—not even with Dante's money. White is such an impractical color; I spill stuff way too easily.

"I'm sorry I didn't offer," Dante remarks, lifting his drink in a toast. It's the first thing he's said since threatening the driver earlier, and his voice sounds weird, off-beat.

Unenthused, I lift my drink in response but don't say anything. I just focus on the ice cubes swirling around the glass, clinking against the side.

I don't know what to do now; nothing is going as I had planned.

Dante takes the seat beside me, pulling me into his lap and wrapping me in those muscular arms of his. I don't fight him; just put my glass down before I spill on the furniture.

"Hey," he says softly, lifting my chin to face him. "I'm sorry, *Tesoro*. It's complicated," he tries again, but the vague apology does little to stir me. I remain still, unmoving, in his arms. "Say something," Dante pleads, caressing my cheek gently.

"What do you want me to say?" My voice is soft but strained. I know I should be more understanding, especially since I know what line of work he's in. But I can't help but feel sorry for myself. This was supposed to be my big moment...

"I don't know. Anything. I hate feeling this distant from you."

I finally look at him, at the sincerity in his eyes. He's trying, I know he is—I can see how hard this is for him.

Still, I wish he would tell me what is causing him all this turmoil.

"I just wanted to make you happy." My lip quivers. *Don't cry; don't cry, Danica.* Easier said than done.

"I know, my love. And you do, you make me so happy." Sweetly, Dante kisses the side of my head. "I'm sorry I reacted like such a jackass. I know you've put in a lot of work."

"Why not Vegas?" The question repeats in my head as it has since we arrived.

Dante sighs heavily. "It was long ago. Turf war drama. You know I don't like to burden you with work stuff."

"But this isn't your turf."

"We used to have some business here. Just before my dad died. Things went south pretty quickly. Long story short, the Feras were banned from ever entering Vegas again."

"You could've just said that from the start. But that's not everything, is it?"

He's holding out on me but I have no idea why. The last time he kept a secret from me, I almost lost him for good. I had no idea where to begin searching when he got kidnapped, locked up, and left for dead in that warehouse.

Just thinking back to the Ricci incident last year makes the hairs on my neck stand upright. I never want to relive that period again. Wondering whether Dante was alive or dead was pure hell.

"That's the important part." He smiles faintly and I accept that there is nothing to gain from pushing him further. He'll tell me when he's ready. I hope so.

It's my turn to sigh as I rest my head against Dante's chest, listening to his heartbeat—my favorite sound.

"So, who's in charge back home while we're gallivanting in Vegas?" Dante changes the subject, stroking my back in lazy patterns.

"I told Carlo not to let anyone in the gates and to tell people you're sick if they ask," I answer with a grin, proud of my detailed plans.

But I'm the only one who's proud. Alarmed, Dante jumps up so fast that I topple off his lap onto the couch. "What? No. Danica. I never take sick days. What will everyone think? I need to phone Carlo."

I pull him back down onto the seat. "You will do no such thing. Why are you so obsessed with this perfect image? You're always trying to please others, but what about Dante? What does *he* want?"

My darling boy doesn't answer. He just looks at his phone on the table and back to me, weighing up his options.

"Hey, look at me, baby. You can go back to being the fearless Don Fera next week. But can we please enjoy our Valentine's together already?"

Dante sighs and kicks off his shoes. "Fine, but we're not leaving this room," he insists.

It can't all be lost, surely? I take a deep breath, gathering my thoughts.

"Well, we don't have to leave the room to have fun." I manage a grin, changing the tone. It is taking too much energy to keep up the sulking, it's not like me.

"Is that so?" Dante's expression instantly switches to intrigued as I drop my hand to his lap, lazily tracing the outline of his still-resting cock, his need to phone back home suddenly completely forgotten.

"When was the last time you were allowed to come, Don Fera?" I ask, firming up my grip.

Dante gasps.

At least there is still one sure way to get Don Fera out of his head and into the physical realm...

CHAPTER THREE

SONJA

DANTE...

My hardness grows by the second as I kneel on the plush carpet, naked, my eyes closed. Fresh out of the shower, soaped and dried as my Queen ordered, I sit back on my heels, awaiting her next command.

Keeping my hands flat on my thighs as instructed becomes a full-time struggle, but I know I must wait; I must not touch my dick no matter how difficult it is to resist. My patience will be rewarded.

"Sit up, baby." Danica finally addresses me, and I lift my body upright, keeping my knees on the carpet. Her voice instantly soothes me; I know I can trust her.

"Eyes closed," she reminds me and I take a deep breath to steady my increasing heartbeat, driven by anticipation and lust.

I remain in darkness as Danica fastens the familiar collar around my neck. It's not the plain black one I normally wear under my clothes—it's the martingale collar with the adjustable metal chain looped around the front.

The chain feels cold against my collarbone, and I shiver involuntarily in a ripple that goes all the way from my neck to my dick, perking it up even more. The anticipation is almost unbearable. Almost.

"Come with me. Keep 'em closed," Danica orders, her voice slow and sultry, commanding.

She pulls the front of the chain and the collar tightens around my neck, digging into my skin, choking me in its familiar way. I like how it feels, the security of it, the reminder—I am owned.

Like the pet I am for her, I crawl behind Danica, letting her guide my knees over the soft carpet, neck first, until I gasp for breath, my windpipe struggling against the chain. There is nothing to think about, to focus on, except the next step, and the next.

More attuned to my body than I am myself, Danica instantly notices when the chain pulls too taut. The metal immediately goes slack and I cough, desperately trying to restore my breathing to a normal rhythm.

"You know I love it when you're being a good boy," Danica coos in my ear, hunching over to whisper in my ear.

She smells of expensive perfume, I still don't know which one—it's fresh with a hint of citrus.

Just like that, I melt, an involuntary groan escaping my lips.

"Up!" Danica orders, the toe of her shoe pressing against my shoulder, pushing me back onto my heels. "Open them."

The darkness dissipates and Danica slowly comes into view as my eyes adjust to the light.

Like a dog, I whimper softly, knowing I'm not allowed to speak without being spoken to. But, my god, she looks stunning!

I've never seen this outfit before. It's a harness of some sort, weaving over her voluptuous curves like a one-piece swimming costume made of red leather straps. It doesn't cover anything; it just digs into her large breasts top and bottom, around her ass, the V nestled between her thick thighs—just a long belt snaking around her pale skin. I can't stop staring.

"Do you like what you see, puppy?" my Queen asks, letting me admire the full view.

I am virtually drooling. "You look sensational!"

"Do you want me?" One of her favorite questions, one I will never tire of answering.

"So much. More than ever." It is the god-honest truth. My thoughts have all been replaced by simple needs, simple wants...

Danica's mischievous eyes glow as she watches me closely. "I can tell. Sonja is very excited."

I cock my head sideways. "Who is *Sonja*?"

Danica moves closer, pressing my fully erect cock against my stomach with her shoe, pinning it down to my body. "I've decided this little one is called Sonja from now on." She smiles, amused with her little games. "What do you think?"

"Why Sonja?" I'm taken aback by the bizarre notion of giving my dick a female name.

"Why not?" Danica increases her foot's pressure on my sensitive flesh and I moan loudly. It feels so good to be touched down there, even if it is by those pointy black shoes.

"Sonja," I repeat, looking down at my trapped cock, desperate and needy. I never thought of naming it before. A name like Sonja seems emasculating in a way, but I suppose that's the point. It's embarrassing really, but Danica knows I enjoy the humiliation...only if it comes from her, though.

"Does Sonja want some release today?" She grinds her shoe into my sensitive dickhead and a jolt of pain shoots through my body, flooding my system with dopamine. It's exhilarating!

Danica knows it drives me feral when she hurts me like that. Our contract makes it clear that I want her to hurt me until my brain goes quiet, amongst other things.

"Please, Miss. I'll do whatever you want." I'm whining. Only Danica can make me whine like this. The power she has over me is unmatched.

My words are true—I will do anything she wants, physically. My mind, my mind is a slower process...I'm not used to giving anyone my mind. So many years of putting up the walls, locking everyone out, forcing myself to be strong so the family could survive.

"Whatever I want? Hmm...I have many wants." Danica releases my trapped cock and it springs free, fully erect now. Then, she grabs my collar and pulls me off my knees until I tower over her, more than a foot taller, but completely subservient.

As Danica's hand wraps around my cock, I grunt loudly, almost collapsing to my knees again. I'm moments from leaking pre-cum onto her fingers, I can't help myself.

"Is someone desperate?" Her Teacher-voice is so patronizing, so sweet—it drives me wild.

"Please, Miss," I whimper, standing as still as I can, holding my breath. I know she likes it when I'm vocal for her, but it's something I still need to get used to. Moaning isn't something I usually do, not like this. *A man must be a man,* my dad's voice torments me as it often does.

"Hmm...I have a surprise for you," Danica says, eyeing her watch.

Hand firmly around my cock, she drags me to the window where thick blackout curtains hide us from the buzzing world below. But not for long. With a single press of a button, Danica opens our private world to the fading light of the spectacular sunset.

I gasp, frozen as the wall becomes completely see-through. Logically, I know they can't see me, but the feeling of being on display overwhelms all logic.

"Isn't it beautiful, baby? I heard the sunsets in Vegas are to die for!" Danica exclaims excitedly, hand still firmly around my cock. "Just look at that." She keeps me there, eyes locked on the view as the neon lights start sparkling against the ever-darkening backdrop. *Oh, Vegas.* We used to have so much fun here.

I want to watch the sunset, to share her enthusiasm, but I'm painfully aware of my own needs. Especially when Danica's fingers start to move, massaging my skin, toying with the tip of my cock, the sensitive bit just beneath it—she knows all my spots, all my hidden buttons. Just a single touch and I'm hers.

Danica is teasing me; I know she won't let me come—not yet. But my dick is stupidly hopeful, pushing into her hand as it searches for more friction.

I don't get far. "Down, Sonja!" Just like that, Danica releases my erection and smacks it with the back of her hand—hard.

Instantly, I double over in pain, falling onto the couch behind me with a loud grunt. *Oh god, it hurts.* But in a good way. It's exactly what I need. The pain feels different in a controlled context like this; when I know I can stop at any moment.

"Sit up straight, boy," Danica demands as she climbs onto the couch, heels and all, legs spread. She doesn't seem bothered by the glass wall behind her, or the fact that she's wearing very little clothing.

But I don't spare any more thoughts for the view or the sunset living out its final minutes. Danica's pussy is mere inches from my face as she fans open her nether lips with two fingers, exposing her clit for me.

With my eyes glued to her crotch, I lick my lips, trying to catch a whiff of her scent. But she's freshly showered too; I get nothing but faint soap and lust. It doesn't make me want her any less.

"You hungry, baby?" she teases.

"Very. Please..." I whine, lips quivering. She knows how much I love her taste; how much I love the privilege of bringing her pleasure.

Danica presses her knee to my torso, pushing me back against the couch.

"Hands on my ass," she orders, and I happily grab her round cheeks, pulling her into me.

"There you go, darling. Make me come." She throws her head back in a loud gasp as my mouth finds its target, adding, "If you're good, maybe you'll get a reward of your own."

Hungry for her, I sink my tongue into her center, my lips closing around her clit. Danica shudders violently, I can feel it. She tangles her fingers in my curls, pulling my hair until it hurts, but I don't move from my post.

I know her body intimately—every sound, every twitch, every tremble. Listening carefully, I let her guide me to her pleasure, finding the spots that make her knees weak and her wetness spread, spread for me to lap it up breathlessly like a thirsty man at an oasis.

"Don't you dare stop, baby," Danica moans, grinding her cunt into my face as I pick up pace. I hold onto her ass for dear life as I eat her out, licking and nibbling and sucking until she pulls my hair painfully, moans intensifying to loud calls of desire, threatening to spill over into screams of pleasure.

But I don't stop, I wouldn't dare. I don't want to either, not until I get the reward: her entire body shaking in ecstasy, declaring "I'm coming!" for the world to hear. Even then, I don't slow down, not until she slaps me across the face, demanding "Enough!"

I finally pull away, licking her wetness off my lips, savoring the taste. *Success!*

Breathless, Danica collapses on my lap—my cock between us, trapped by our bodies—as she pushes forward for a kiss.

I kiss her back, eager for her lips, her tongue—I want it all! Most of all, I want her to taste her pleasure on my lips.

"Hmm, you did so well, baby. Thank you." My Queen smiles when she pulls away, touching my cheek in that affectionate manner of hers.

My cock twitches between us, ruining the innocence of the moment.

"Aww, does Sonja want some attention too?" Danica coos, and I blush. My dick's always had a life of its own, but never more colorful than since Danica came around. I guess it's fitting that it got a name of its own too.

"Sonja can't resist you, what can I say?" I shrug, averting my eyes, suddenly self-conscious. How does she make me feel like such a little boy? *Oh, Dio mio.*

As night falls outside, Danica gets up from the couch, careful not to impale me with her heels on the way down. (Not that I would mind.) It's my turn to moan as she takes my cock between those beautiful lips, licking my flesh back to full hardness.

"All nice and wet, just how I like it." She slobbers more saliva on my erection before abruptly spitting me out, drawing a pained cry of protest from my lips.

"Don't move," Danica tells me, and I keep perfectly still while she grabs my shoulders and lowers herself onto my saliva-covered cock with steely concentration. "I want you inside me"—another one of her favorite lines, and one of mine too.

I bite my lip, holding my breath, as the Goddess in red takes me in, all of me. There is no greater feeling, I'm convinced.

When my cock is buried inside her to the hilt, she just sits there, unmoving on my lap.

Keeping my gaze, Danica throws her arms around my neck and pulls me closer, her large breasts squishing against my chest. Her lips find mine and I kiss her back with blurred passion.

Without breaking away, her lips still on mine, Danica slowly pushes herself up on her knees, letting my cock slide out just a bit before plunging onto my lap again.

Her moans mix with mine as she rides me. Oh god, I know I won't last long like this. She's left me on the edge so many times, I'm desperate for a release.

Danica bounces up and down my cock, grinding her hips sensually, her hands holding my face. She stares into my soul and I let her, smiling stupidly as she fucks me into oblivion.

My pleasure starts building quickly. Too quickly. It takes every ounce of willpower to keep it from spilling over, and even then, I'm on the brink of failing.

"Please..." I moan, no, beg.

"Tell me what you want, darling. Use your words," Danica demands, even though there is nothing mysterious about my needs.

"I'm close...Please, Miss. Please give me permission," I cry, clenching to keep the flood at bay.

"How close?" She smirks, contemplating the tortured look on my face.

"Please!" I let out an exasperated howl. *I can't hold it.* I don't dare come without permission, but I can't!

"Poor baby. You've been so good. You have permission. Come for me. Inside me. I want to feel you..." As she speaks, Danica rides me faster and faster, bouncing on my dick until I explode violently inside her, pumping her full of my cum.

An uninhibited roar escapes my lips, a roar that Danica kisses hungrily, devouring my lips as my body convulses in ecstasy beneath her.

But she doesn't get up; she keeps me inside—sticky and sensitive. I pant wildly, gasping for air as the overstimulation burns through my body. It feels like an eternity before my Queen shows mercy and stops rocking on top of me.

When I open my eyes, I find her smiling at me, regarding me with intensity. Tired but happily spent, I smile back as she strokes my hair, kissing my temples while telling me how much she loves me.

"I love you. So much," I respond as I kiss her again, holding her close, our satisfied bodies merging into a single mess of limbs.

"Should we move this to the bed?" Danica suggests, kissing my nose sweetly.

I nod, waiting for her to get up. But she doesn't.

"You're staying inside though," Danica adds with a huge grin.

"How—?" I start, but slowly piece together what she has in mind.

"Ah. Yes, Ma'am." I lock my hands under her ass and pick us both off the couch, lifting from my calves.

Holding onto my neck tightly, Danica wraps her legs around my waist for the ride, my cum leaking from her cunt down my thighs.

Behind us, the fresh night sky sparkles with possibility and temptation...

**UNSENT LETTER #1

Dear you,

I know I will never send this letter, but perhaps I can finally make sense of what happened if I write it down.

All I know is that I need the story to exist, the real version; the one I could never tell anyone.

Even after almost five years, I can't stop thinking about you, about what could have been. Perhaps I'm writing this more for me than for you.

Let's sneak away, you said that day, this is boring. You had that look in your eyes, that mischievous glint that would get me into so much trouble still. I would follow those eyes anywhere, and I did.

Hesitating only momentarily, I took your outstretched hand, and we slipped through the cracks. Down hidden passages and sneaky doors, into the world of sex and drugs and pure desire. It was all new to me, but with your hand in mine, I felt brave.

Our fathers were immersed in the negotiations; they didn't notice us running off, barely legal, with the whole of Vegas at our feet. Armed and dangerous but, oh, so stupid still.

I was still a virgin, I knew nothing of those dark worlds, the depraved clubs you navigated like a proud guide. Even though you were a few months younger than me, you had lived so much already. You wanted to show me. It is time, you said.

We were in Utopia, but neither of us cared about the clubs or the naked bodies on offer at the buffet. No, I was there for you and only you. The way you looked at me, held my hand, touched me—I knew you felt the same. We weren't kids anymore like when we first met, when you shared your secret collection of beautiful poems with me on a rainy Tuesday morning.

Had I any sense, I would have said no, not have taken your hand, stayed behind. But the reckless abandonment you inspired in me scared and excited me in equal measure.

Why does forbidden fruit taste so good?

CHAPTER FOUR

ENCHANTED

DANICA...

You got this, gurl. Tonight is the night, I wordlessly try to hype up my reflection, sighing deeply as I apply the finishing touches to my look with a deep-red lipstick.

The pep talk does little to put me at ease, the nerves still gnawing at my spine. But I try to push it all down, willing the smile onto my face.

"Stunning!" Dante declares as I exit the bathroom, dressed and ready for our special Valentine's show—the whole reason we are here in the first place. I got us tickets to an exclusive kinky burlesque show all the way from Berlin. In Vegas, for one night only.

Oh, the things money can buy. Especially when you remove the guilt of spending stupid amounts on stupid things. *If my broke-ass teenage self could see me now...*

Initially, I didn't think we'd get tickets but Adira had some Domme connections in high places; she pulled some strings and got us VIP seats. The perfect Valentine's gift...

And then, at the last minute, Dante had almost ruined it all with his refusal to leave the room. No amount of pain and pleasure could put his mind at ease. I'd tried all night until we both passed out in an exhausted stupor, the cum sufficiently emptied from our bodies.

But this morning, Dante had surprised us both by agreeing to go, as long as we found a mask to hide his face. It was a good solution, one that would hopefully allow me to finally see the enchanting city lights I'd only admired from our room.

Forcing my attention to the present, I study Dante's outfit, whistling at him like I'm a construction worker catcalling some woman on the street. The blush it brings to his cheeks is so cute.

"You look pretty good yourself," I remark as I kiss him, the fancy lipstick keeping its promise not to smear.

Dante is dressed in all black: tight pants, ankle-high boots, a matching belt, and a vest concealed under his favorite leather jacket. He initially wanted to wear one of his usual uptight collared shirts, but I'd argued relentlessly until he gave up and pulled on the vest I had put out for him. It is a good look on him, even if he doesn't agree. It makes him look like some biker bad-boy.

A simple black Venetian mask covers the top half of his face, hiding his identity and completing the ensemble.

"Give us a twirl," Dante asks, taking my hand. Happy to oblige, I turn around with my arms stretched out, my all-black knee-length dress fanning out around me.

This is such a fun outfit; I like how I look. The top half is basically a corset, pushing my large breasts into a sizable cleavage while a long black skirt flows down to my ankles. My shoulder-length hair is pinned up all elegant with sparkly earrings dangling beside my face. Spiky heels complete the look, matched to my handbag like I've been fancy all my life, not just since I met Dante.

But he loves me whether I'm fancy or not. Our connection runs way deeper than pedigree anyway. Right from the start, something drew me to him; I knew there was someone else beneath the hard exterior, beneath the scary mafia boss persona.

"So ravishing, I don't even want to share you. Do we have to go?" Dante tries one more time, but my resistance keeps firm.

"Absolutely! Flattery won't get you anywhere this time, Don Fera. Now get your stuff. I don't want to be late."

"It's Vegas, *Tesoro*. Stuff always starts late," he tries to reassure me.

"It's my first time...I want to experience it all!" Excited, I take his hand and lead him to the elevator before he can change his mind. I may be the one that contractually holds control, but I'm not the one physically capable of throwing someone over their shoulder to get their way.

In the elevator, Dante hesitates, finger hovering over the ground floor button. "Isn't Emilio coming?"

"No, darling. Tickets for this thing were damn near impossible to get. Emilio can have tonight off." I press the number myself and we start our descent from the sky...I doubt Emilio would enjoy the show anyway. Not that I know (or want to know) what the old man is into.

"I don't like going anywhere without Emilio." Dante shifts his weight from one leg to the other, twisting the rings on his fingers without looking at them. His restlessness is obvious.

"So co-dependent, if you ask me," I try to lighten the mood with sarcasm, but it's not helping. For the umpteenth time, I wonder if we should just stay inside. But we're so close, no. I want it to be special. *It's just one night.*

Dante's face remains stern. "Danica, security isn't funny. I vowed to protect you at all times."

"Wasn't I the one who had to rescue your ass last time—when you got taken by the enemy?" I remind him.

"Yes, and I am eternally grateful to you. But that's my point. It's dangerous. It's always dangerous."

The elevator dings and the doors slide open onto the lavish hotel lobby, cutting the conversation short.

"Keep your mask on; we'll be okay. Nobody knows who you are here. They sure don't know who I am because I've never been here."

Dante grumbles something unintelligible but I pay him no mind. He tends to default to "no" when new things are concerned. I usually blame his age. Luckily he has me to keep him young, even if he doesn't always agree with my notion of adventure.

A car is waiting for us outside, but not the same one as before. *Fuck those guys.* As we slide into the back seat, I'm nervously excited for our night. I'm finally ready for the next step...I have no idea how Dante will react, but I sincerely hope it'll be better than when he realized he was in Vegas.

I wish he would tell me the whole story of his beef with this city, but the way he flinches at the mere mention of it makes it clear that it's painful. My guess is probably some long-lost love who got away. I find myself wondering who she might be (if she exists in the first place, that is).

I know I'm not Dante's usual type—I'm just a rough-around-the-edges ordinary girl from a lower-middle-class family with a shitty public school background. But a Vegas girl? She must have been spectacular!

Determined, I try to force the thought out of my head. I don't like getting jealous. Yet it's a feeling I find myself grappling with so often. Who could blame me? I'm so used to things being taken from me, to always losing, or never being enough in the first place—I need Dante to be *mine*.

I know I have no reason to worry; Dante always assures me that I'm all he wants, that I'm the only one who understands him. And I believe him.

The drive to the show isn't far—nothing around here is really far, I'm realizing. But it's long enough for me to get a good view of the Strip. *This place is unreal!*

Like a woman enchanted, I'm completely entranced by the views blurring past outside my window. Neon signs of every color imaginable stretch into the distance, creating a kaleidoscope of brilliance against the dark desert sky.

I can't believe this is the same city we arrived in yesterday, that nighttime can transform anything this dramatically. No book or movie can convey the sheer magnificence of being here in real life.

Beside me with his hand on my lap, Dante still looks worried. Well, the lower half of his face does at least. I can tell by how he bites his lip, by how he clenches his other fist. I'm sure he'll relax once we get to the show. Maybe he'll even feel *inspired*.

Besides, I find it hard to fear anything with Dante by my side. I know he'll always protect me, no matter what. Nobody has ever been there for me the way he has.

But Danica, what about your parents—parents will do anything for their kids, even die, the never-ending game show host in my head shouts as the neon passes by. Not my parents. Maybe for my brothers, for the sadistic twins who took pleasure in ruining my childhood. But definitely not for me.

Poor little Danica, making a fuss about a stupid dead dog. So what if I'd almost died along with my only friend, that majestic black Labrador with the wet nose? *Just hush Danica, don't ruin their perfect future.* No, my parents never protected me.

But Danica, what about your ex? You were together for so long. You gave up everything for him...surely he would've protected you?

Shut up already! That fucking voice is driving me insane.

But it doesn't shut up. No, it chooses to bring up that asshole's cheating; now, when we're on our way to our special evening, it reminds me how I was never good enough for anyone. Used, discarded, scarred...poor little Danica is acting out again; best silence her or, even better—ignore her.

Dante was the first person who treated me differently, who actually saw me. He would do anything for me, no matter how broken I am. He treats me like the Queen I was told I'd never be, not just some white trash kid at a fancy school where she didn't belong. *Someone get the "povo" out of here,* they used to tease.

But Dante keeps his promises, he looks after me. He only withdraws at times when he can't handle himself. I've learned that those moments are not about me. He has a lot of repressed emotions..

The car pulls up in front of a grand building with a dark red sign glittering above the entrance, and I force my chaotic thoughts back in line.

Tonight's the night, Danica.

I'll really do it this time; I will. No chickening out again like before.

I want to remember every detail of tonight, of this special occasion.

But nothing would ever be the same after tonight.

And not for the reasons I had planned.

Silly me. I had no idea what I was getting us into...

CHAPTER FIVE

UNEASE

DANTE...

A lthough I've never been to this venue, it feels the same as any other of its kind I've frequented in my youth. The same dingy lighting, the same long corridors, the well-dressed bouncers at the door, the mysterious doors leading to mysterious rooms with mysterious people.

"Come on, old man, hurry up." Danica tugs at my jacket in the hopes of making me walk faster. But I stop dead in my tracks and pull her back instead, overpowering her effortlessly.

She lets out a surprised shriek as I lift her face close to mine. "I'm not *old*," I snarl, much to Danica's amusement. She may be my Domme, but our dynamic has always enjoyed more nuance, more complexity, than such binary roles. My Queen can be a bit of a brat sometimes, and I often have to put my foot down. But we both know she holds the ultimate power.

"I'm just teasing. Down boy." She kisses my nose and I let her go, growling in mock protest. "Now hurry, please." Danica's off again and I follow her begrudgingly, looking around every few steps to make sure we're not being followed. It feels wrong to be here again, in this city.

We are escorted through the venue by a man with a gun instead of a personality, and he silently leads us through the maze of sin and seduction. He makes me feel ill at ease; the only man with a gun I want escorting us is Emilio, and he isn't anywhere nearby.

We shouldn't be here—the thought jolts me into a bumpy ride down memory lane as I follow Danica through the dark corridors.

We were so young back then, so hopeful. There was only one person I'd wanted by my side as we set the world on fire. But the world knew that we'd be trouble together; that it would be better to keep us apart. It's been so long since I thought of those amber eyes, that playful grin...

Pinching my arm, Danica pulls me back from my nostalgia. We've arrived.

I look around the intimate room with no more than 15 round tables encircling a cylindrical glass chamber that serves as the stage. It all feels so painfully familiar.

Inside the enclosed glass, the warm-up "acts" are doing their thing, some tasteful whipping of willing slaves for the audience to feast on in 360-degree voyeurism.

As soon as we sit down, a waiter appears, and I order two drinks from the man dressed only in gold underpants. I'm unbelievably thirsty, though I need the drinks to soothe more than just my thirst.

"See, isn't this nice?" Danica smiles, putting her hand on mine. I find now comfort in the gesture, despite her intent. I wish I could share her excitement for the show, but I'm counting the seconds until we're back in the safety of our room.

Crossing my arms over my chest, I don't bother translating my response for her as I grumble my objections in Italian.

"Hey! Look here, baby." Danica pulls my face towards her. "It's going to be fine."

Before I can reply, a glass drops behind us, shattering on the floor. On instinct, I jump up, almost knocking over the candle on our table. *Cazzo!*

Danica pulls me back to my seat. "Jesus, Dante. You're so jittery. I promise we're going straight home after the show."

"Hmm."

As soon as our drinks arrive, I down the first one in a single gulp.

You'd better listen to her, Dante. Stop being such a pussy. It's my dad's voice again, critical as always. *You're supposed to be the head of the Fera family, start acting like it!*

For once I agree with my dad. Why can't I get my fucking nerves under control?

But then I remember that burn on my face—both from the punch and the embarrassment. I remember Emilio dragging me out of there kicking and screaming before I could get us all killed. I remember the final look I ever saw in those enigmatic amber eyes...before they left forever.

No! No more.

It's too hot in here; I can't breathe. Restless, I pull off my jacket and chuck it over the open chair at our table. It does little to relieve my sweaty palms.

"Why can't they turn up the AC in here?" I mutter. "We should talk to someone about the lack of climate control."

"Sure. Happy Valentine's, by the way." Danica sighs as she pushes the ice in her cocktail around with a straw. She looks miserable. And it's all my fault. The realization crashes down on me like a ton of bricks.

Forcing myself to be more present, I take her hand. "I'm sorry, *Tesoro*. I'll relax," I promise her, but we both know it's just words. "But first, more alcohol." I wave down the waiter and order another double whiskey.

Danica shakes her head to decline a refill; she's still good with her first whatever-she-drinks. Her order always changes depending on her mood. *Typical Danica.* Always so carefree, so adventurous.

If only she knew the potential danger that lurked in the shadows of this sinister city. But then again, her world hadn't been as tainted with death and disaster as mine had. The only time she's in danger is because of me.

My fingers drift to the fresh scar on her arm as they often do, tracing the ugly outline the knife had left on her skin. The scar makes me want to break something, someone. It reminds me how much she loves me, how she'd do anything to try and save me, even throw herself into harm's way. But more than that, it feeds the guilt. If I hadn't gotten kidnapped, if I hadn't been born into this life, Danica wouldn't have had to come and save me, getting stabbed in the process.

It wasn't too bad of a cut. Nothing a few stitches and some time wouldn't heal. But it still blemished her perfect skin, torturing me with the knowledge that I failed to protect her. Too many people have gotten hurt already.

I sigh, twisting the rings that adorn four fingers on each hand. So many dead now—my parents, my grandparents, my wife...I will not wear a ring for Danica's memory too.

I want her to feel as safe as she makes me feel. And not because she literally saved my life when I was betrayed and abducted, chained bleeding to a rusty metal chair for days without any hope of survival.

It's about more than my body; Danica calms my mind too. When I submit to her, all the darkness, all the guilt, the anger...it all goes away—even if just for a bit. She's the only one who sees me, the real me.

But even Danica doesn't know the skeletons I'd buried in Vegas.

Unable to shake the uneasy feeling, I shift around in my seat, trying to focus on the scene playing out in front of me. Some small-dicked man in a dog mask is getting walked over by a slim-waisted-large-busted woman in leather pants. It was the kind of show you'd expect to see in a place like this.

The last time I saw a show like that in Vegas, I had been so drunk. Just like all those times before as well, even though neither of us were of legal drinking age yet. We ran around the Strip, causing havoc, feeling fearless and unstoppable. Until they'd stopped us...

"You're so far away, baby. What's on your mind?" Danica asks, gently putting her hand on my thigh.

She looks so majestic tonight, as she always does. I hate that the sadness on her face is because of me. Silently, I berate myself for not being a better partner, the man she deserves.

"I'm sorry, my love. I'm just feeling a bit tired." I smile faintly, the real words I'm supposed to tell her submerged too deeply to articulate. Where would I even start?

It doesn't even matter anymore. I'm not who I was back then. No, 19-year-old Dante was foolish, young, horny. Nothing could ever have come from it. It was good that we were interrupted before it could go any further.

With a strained smile, I put my hand over Danica's and bring it to my lips, kissing her soft skin. My Queen smiles, lighting up the face that has been shrouded in darkness since our arrival. I silently vow to get my emotions in check so I can stop spoiling her carefully laid plans, whatever they may be.

I pull her closer, chair and all, to put my arm around her. With a sigh, I breathe in her hair, careful not to mess it up. Her familiar citrus scent calms me, pushing down the demons.

Things are different now. We'll be okay, I repeat to myself again, hoping the words will sink in, that they'll calm me.

But they don't.

****UNSENT LETTER #2**

We drank the night away as the music grew louder, the lights dimmer. I knew we should get back to the negotiations, that the families would be looking for us, yet I wanted nothing more than to spend an eternity lost in your playful gaze.

I wasn't used to this feeling, to this wanting. I've had my fill of damsels throwing themselves at my feet, desperate, convinced they'll bear the new heir to the Fera dynasty. But none of them made me feel like this, this fluttering that rose in my stomach whenever you crashed into my orbit.

When we were younger, I looked forward to our meetings way more than I should've. But I put it down to the loneliness, to wanting a good friend. But this time, this time I knew for sure I wanted to be more than friends.

Before us, a kinky chorus of women in various stages of undress shook and jiggled on stage, baring all on a silver platter I let pass by. The menu item I wanted wasn't listed, it was taboo. We knew it was. Our families were reluctant business partners at best, rivals according to some.

Yet I could not resist you. When you pressed your lips against mine in that first stolen kiss as the lights went dark and the people clapped...in that moment, I lost a part of my soul that I would never get back.

CHAPTER SIX

TAKEN

Danica...

E yes locked on the female performer's sinuous movements, I'm completely captivated by the show on stage. Her body sways in the soft, seductive glow of the lights, the air thick with perfume and sweat.

I'm so mesmerized that I don't notice the strangers until it's too late, until I feel something hard press uncomfortably into my back.

Fuck.

A whisper, close and harsh, chills my ear. "No sudden moves." My breath catches, and my skin prickles with dread. The realization dawns slowly, cold and heavy—it's a gun against my back.

My heart is pounding and not in a good way; I don't know what to do. This isn't the suburbs; this isn't a TV drama. This is real, and I am unprepared.

On stage, the performance continues, a beautiful dance of dominance and submission. The dim room casts no shadows except for the soft spotlight that highlights the naked bodies entwined in their glass-walled world. The audience is oblivious to our predicament, eyes glued to their entertainers, applause rising as the act concludes.

Without turning my head, I regard Dante from the corner of my eye, watching as the two thugs in fancy suits pull him out of his chair—not violently, but forcefully enough. He catches my eye and mouths something that looks like "Stay calm."

Some fucking advice that is.

Around us, the clapping continues, the applause a surreal soundtrack to our nightmare.

"Let her go," Dante threatens in a low voice, but even he can't argue with a concealed weapon to his back. One of the men whispers something to him in Italian and Dante stops fighting. My language skills have progressed to a basic understanding, but it is too noisy with the clapping to make out anything more than the familiar cadence of his native tongue.

"Do what they say, *Tesoro*," Dante tells me, reaching for my hand but one of the goons smacks it away. "They won't hurt you," he adds, but I don't believe him, although I so badly want to.

It's my turn to get up, but my legs don't move how they should; nothing does. Even as I wipe my clammy hands on my dress, they still feel slippery. *What the fuck is going on?* Panic claws at my throat.

We're escorted out of the room, not through the main entrance but down dark, narrow passages with menacing shadows. Footsteps echo ominously in the confined space, as we walk wordlessly to the impending doom I cannot yet fathom.

One of the thugs rips off Dante's mask, throwing it aside. Desperate, I look to my knight for guidance, but his face is a stone wall, an impenetrable fortress—I don't know what's brooding behind those emerald eyes. He's taller, bigger than the men, but we're outnumbered.

Just do something, I silently beg, but I don't know what miracle I'm expecting.

Dante must have had the same idea. Without a word of warning, he suddenly halts abruptly, causing the assailants to stumble. Before his captors can react, Dante turns around and fucks them up, his movements fluid and precise.

Time slows to a crawl and I watch in awe as he disarms the closest assailant with a quick-as-fuck twist of his wrist. The clatter of the gun hitting the floor reverberates in the narrow space.

Dante moves like a panther, fluid and deadly. His fists blur past my head, striking the second gunman with precision. I feel like I'm in some gritty action movie and Dante is the badass MMC who fights like a pro. It would be super-hot if I wasn't fearing for my life right now.

It all happens blisteringly fast and behind me, the third man, stunned, fumbles to react. *This is your moment, Danica.* Now or never.

I don't know how I get my legs to move, but I lift my foot, bringing my heel down hard on the instep of the man behind me. He shouts some Italian curses at me as I spin around and knee him in the groin, just like Emilio taught me in self-defense classes. Conscious me is petrified, frozen in time; unconscious me is in full battle mode, ready to cut a bitch to protect my life, my love.

The fucker screams and lets me go. Fear and adrenaline surge through me but leave me too quickly. I don't know what to do next.

But there's a whole other battle happening too. "Down, Danica!" Dante shouts and I fall to the floor, holding my head protectively as the men fight above me.

I want to close my eyes, but I can't look away. Dante uses one of the doubled-over gunmen as a shield, maneuvering him to block the line of fire. He works quickly, disarming the attackers with brutal efficiency.

There is a lot of shouting in Italian, some in angry English. Dante takes a blow to the face, one to the stomach. I wish I could help him but I lie useless on the floor, shrunken. When I'd saved Dante from the kidnappers before, we'd had an army of guards. But this time we have nobody. And it is all my fault.

Yet Dante fights on, risking everything to save us; he's our only hope.

The struggle for weapons continues in the narrow corridor. I plead to a god I don't believe in to get us through this. I'll never set foot in Vegas again if we can just escape alive, I bargain. I am drowning in guilt but the fear overrides any other emotion, keeping my body stiff, my breath trapped in my throat, shallow.

In the chaos, Dante manages to reach for a discarded weapon on the ground, turning the tide of the confrontation.

"Let's go, Danica," Dante instructs, his eyes locked on the three men backed up against the wall, hands up, their weapons out of reach.

My darling Don looks at me for a second, his gaze softening, reaching out an arm to help me off the floor. Grateful for his familiar touch, I take it and pull myself up, keeping close to him as we back away from the violent suits.

"Take this." He picks up another gun and thrusts the heavy weapon into my hands.

My heart is racing to the point of causing an ache in my chest, struggling to push air through my lungs at a normal rhythm. Adrenaline surges through my veins, as does relief, but we still have to get out of here; we're not saved yet.

Dante's cheek is bleeding, swelling just a little already. But his gaze is made of steel, focused. I can feel the rapid breaths of his body against mine as we slowly walk backward, guns pointed at the perpetrators.

We reach the end of the corridor and Dante shouts: "Run!"

Without question, I follow him, darting around the corner as quickly as I can in these stupid high heels. But we don't get far.

A wall of armed men awaits us around the next corridor.

"*Fermo!*" An unfamiliar voice halts us in our tracks. Even I know that means stop.

"Fuck," Dante mumbles, his shoulders slacking.

"Drop it!" The man in front demands and Dante's weapon clinks on the floor without argument.

"Do as he says, Danica," he tells me, defeated. If I wasn't here, I know he would've considered fighting, but not now. So, I drop my weapon as well; I wouldn't be able to use it anyway. Although I'm decent with a gun, that only counts for the ones I'm comfortable and practiced with.

This time there are too many goons with weapons though. I lose all hope of us surviving Valentine's Day as the bulky men in expensive suits and shiny shoes drag us up some stairs and through another maze of hallways.

They bundle us into a lift, guns pointed at me from all directions. We go almost to the top of the building—just one floor below—before the doors swing open onto a short corridor with a single door.

I try to focus on my breathing and try hard not to panic. But all I want to do is close my eyes and make it go away. *We're so fucked.*

They escort us to the mysterious door and one of the goons knocks, pushing it open when the voice inside permits it. *Oh god, the big boss.* This is never good.

The voice inside belongs to a tall man with broad shoulders and long brown hair hanging down almost to his waist. The kingpin is standing behind his desk, back to us, peering out through the large windows.

The space around us looks like the office of every bad guy in every mafia movie. The walls are draped in deep, rich colors while dim, strategically placed lamps cast a warm glow that dances on the grey walls. It's not dissimilar to Dante's study or Don Greco's. *Is there a preferred color palette for villains, a Mob Boss Pinterest board, or something?*

The room seems to absorb sound, muffling the chaos beyond its confines. I can't hear anything from the club below, not even the clapping or the music from the other floors.

In one corner, a mahogany desk stands as the focal point. A big screen filled with CCTV footage is mounted on the wall just above the desk, showing various areas of the club.

Around us, the walls are covered in elaborate artwork depicting sex scenes in various stages—naked body parts wherever you look, some tasteful, others crude.

We're pushed down on the leather chairs facing the desk, forced into the seats as the master of this castle stares out over the city. Without turning around, the man sighs heavily, cracking his knuckles. *Oh, fuck. This can't be good.*

The tension in the room is thick; electric. I want someone to say something, but I'm petrified of what they will say. There is nowhere to run now.

I look at Dante but his face gives nothing away.

Should've, could've, would've—in hindsight, this is all my fault.

Oh god, I don't want to die like this.

CHAPTER SEVEN

GHOST

DANTE...

My eyes dart around the room, calculating, as I try to find an escape, but there is no move that won't risk killing us both. The ambush in the hallway was risky enough. I shouldn't have gambled with Danica's life. But I knew I could take them.

This time, we stand no chance of escape. We are trapped. And I still don't know by whom.

My heart is pounding, adrenaline rushing through my core. Trying to calm myself, I scan the well-dressed man before us. His back is still turned to us, even after several long minutes of uncomfortable silence. The boss of this establishment, I assume, but I still have no idea who he is, or what he wants with us.

When the long-haired man finally speaks, a chill races down my spine in an uncontrollable shiver. *Fuck!*

"My, my, my," the familiar voice says—his words slow, deliberate—and I freeze. "A Fera in Vegas? And not just any Fera. *You?* Hmm...Never thought anyone would be so foolish."

I know that voice. I shouldn't but I do. Even after all this time.

No. It can't be?

The mysterious man by the window turns around slowly and I find myself face-to-face with a demon I thought I'd buried long ago. I would recognize those amber eyes at any age.

Our gaze locks and the world disappears. I know he's peering into my soul, but I can't look away, I'm desperate to do the same.

"Alessio..." I breathe in barely a whisper, my stare transfixed on the man in the elegant charcoal suit with the open shirt. A tasteful golden teardrop earring dangles from his left ear, catching my eye, as I take stock of how he's changed, of the small scar running along his sharp jawline. There is a streak of grey in those shiny locks that are way longer than I remember, and his gaze looks more tired, but it's unmistakably him.

I squirm in my seat as he walks over to us, those playfully dangerous eyes holding mine hostage. "Hello, darling," our host says with a smile, affectionately brushing my bruised cheek, the drying blood.

Oh god!

And just like that, it all comes rushing back—all the pent-up emotions, the unfinished business, the desire. My breath refuses to leave my lungs, still frozen. His presence is overwhelming my senses, short-circuiting my wires.

"What's going on here? Do you know this dude?" Danica demands, still on high alert.

"Oh, we go way back." Alessio laughs, keeping a mysterious air as he sits down on top of the desk, facing us. His proximity is enough to drive me mad. I can smell his cologne—Aramis. Surely it can't still be the same. But I know it is. *That smell, Jesus.*

"What does that mean?" Danica asks.

"We knew each other when we were young," I say through pursed lips, watching Alessio's every move. My mind refuses to process the fact that it's really him, that he's sitting in front of me, more than double the age he was the last time I saw him. He's only a few months my junior, but he looks much younger than me. He always did have those delicate feminine features—so beautiful, so elegant.

I'm still in shock. For a second, I consider the possibility that I've actually passed out and this is my mind playing tricks on me. I grip the armchair tightly and feel the texture of the leather under my fingertips. It's real.

"Is that a good thing or a bad thing?" Danica asks, darting her concerned gaze from Alessio to me as she tries to size up the threat level.

"Depends on who you ask," Alessio replies.

"Leave us." He waves away the guards who disperse without so much as a question. Commanding an army with a mere gesture—*who has he become?* This is not the reckless teenager with the mischievous streak I used to know.

The men leave without anyone watching them.

"Ah, much better. Now I can have you all to myself, finally. If only we'd had some privacy back then, right?" Alessio laughs. I don't know what to do or how to be. My past and present have collided in a moment that lies trapped in time, unmoving.

"Are you going to kill us?" Danica must be so scared still, I realize. I want to put her at ease but I can't even put myself at ease right now.

"No, *cara mia*. I'm not going to kill you. If I wanted you dead, you wouldn't be sitting here." Alessio smiles, bringing Danica's hand to his lips for a kiss.

"What do you want?" she insists, pulling her hand away, her brow knitted in a frown.

I'm still trying to find my words, but they are all running through my head at a million miles an hour, and none of them have any plans to leave my mouth. Just around and around they go. *Alessio. How is he here?*

"I just want to talk, nothing serious. Maybe finish some unfinished business." He looks at me, winks, and I swear my heart stops.

"I'm confused," Danica declares. And she has every right to be.

"So was I, pretty one. Imagine me going about my day like any other day—you know, running my business—and when I happen to glance up at the screen, I see that familiar tattoo. Your beefcake was smart enough to wear a mask, but the moment he took that jacket off, he was fucked. That band on your arm, remember when we snuck away to get those?"

Alessio rolls up his shirt sleeve to show Danica a matching design on his arm—done in the same ink, at the same time.

"Do you remember, darling?" Alessio asks, rolling his sleeve down again.

They both look at me expectantly, but I still can't find a reply. What do you say? I used to have speeches and speeches prepared for the day we finally met again, but eventually, I gave up thinking the day would ever come.

Now, 25 years later, here we are. And the words have all evaporated, useless.

"What's going on, Dante?" Danica takes my hand, squeezing my fingers in hers—for my comfort or hers, I do not know.

"Oh, he'll come around. The poor man has seen a ghost. Give him some time to adjust."

Alessio gets off the table and bends over before Danica, gently running his fingers over her cheek. "What's your name? Such a beautiful complexion, hmm..." He always did have such a disarming quality, a way of putting you at ease instantly.

But Danica isn't that easily won over, especially not when you just threatened her life. She turns her face, recoiling from him. "Danica," she says simply, confidently. Such a brave one.

"Danica? I like it. Nice to meet you, Danica. As you've heard, I'm Alessio. Alessio Santoro. From the Vegas Santoro family, I would usually add. But Dante already knows that, and the information means nothing to you, I presume? Quite a young thing, aren't you? How old are you?"

"I'm 25, not *that* young." Danica's voice is losing its hostility with every response as Alessio works his charm.

She's always been a great judge of character; I wonder what she'll make of Alessio.

"Hmm, you're as old as our history together. Back then your Romeo was just a wee lad, barely 19, running around the shiny streets of Vegas, ready to set it all ablaze. Perhaps we would've if they hadn't stopped us." Alessio lets out a heavy sigh as he looks at me. We both know he's right—we could've had it all. Maybe in another universe...

"Are you going to kidnap us?" Danica asks.

"Kidnap you? Maybe if bondage is your thing. But no, I'm a lover, not a fighter, *cara mia*. Kidnapping is not really my style." Alessio laughs heartily again, and I can see Danica relaxing a bit, letting her shoulders slump as she exhales slowly.

"I brought you here to protect you, not to harm you. The guns were merely for show, to get you here. I doubt Don Fera would have come willingly. I should've known you'd try to fight anyway. You never did make it easy for yourself, did you?" Alessio sighs.

I can't bring myself to meet his gaze.

"Are you in the mafia too?" Danica asks.

"Something like that," Alessio replies. "Let's just say you can be glad I'm the one who spotted you and not someone else in my family. You have some nerve showing your face in Vegas, Don Fera."

"It's not his fault, he didn't know we were coming here. I wanted to surprise him for Valentine's Day," Danica quickly explains as Alessio watches me intently, eyes burning through me. I feel like I'm 19 again, staring into those carefree amber globes with more questions than answers.

"It seems fate has brought us together after all this time," Alessio declares. "We should celebrate. Whiskey?" He jumps off the desk and heads to the drinks tray near the window.

Danica nods politely and Alessio looks at me expectantly, glass in the hand.

"Francesco?" I ask, incapable of stringing a full sentence together.

"Ah, the Don speaks!" Alessio laughs nonchalantly.

I grit my teeth. "Answer me."

Alessio sighs, tapping his fingers on the table. "All these years apart and you want to know about my brother?"

"Where is he?" I insist. We both know why.

"Don't worry your pretty head, dear. That scumbag isn't here," Alessio answers like it should put me at ease. But I've been looking over my shoulder for Francesco since we arrived, waiting for him to pounce from any and every corner we turn.

Alessio returns to the task at hand without offering any more info. "So, for the second time, whiskey?" he asks, shaking the bottle of Dalmore like it's just an everyday drink instead of a luxury few can afford. It's been a while since I had one of those. Only a fool—or a complete hedonist—would spend that much on a bottle of liquor. I suspect Alessio may be a bit of both, but I don't know who he's become since our last encounter.

Still, my throat is dry and a bit of liquid courage would be useful for the unidentifiable feelings that gnaw at my insides like it's trying to break me apart.

"Double...please," I manage to utter, my voice creaking.

"A double it is. See, was that so hard now?"

His hand brushes against mine as I take the drink. For a moment, we both freeze. Alessio smiles warmly as he holds my gaze. "*Mi sei mancato, amore mio,*" he whispers. *I've missed you, my love.*

I've missed him too. More than I thought I did.

But I don't say anything.

CHAPTER EIGHT

CONFUSED

Danica...

My heartbeat finally slows to its normal rhythm as the adrenaline leaves my veins. Okay, so we're not being kidnapped. *That's something, right?*

But it doesn't help me solve the mystery of what is actually happening right now. I don't know what's going on with Dante; I've never seen him act so weird. Who is this Alessio guy? What's their story?

Questions whirl through my mind like leaves in a storm, but Dante is mute, and Alessio acts like the Joker of the pack, laughing in riddles. They make no sense to me, yet Dante seems to understand every word.

What the fuck is going on?

This clearly isn't the guy Dante was afraid of finding in Vegas; he seems genuinely surprised to see Alessio. Perhaps it's all connected, it must be.

My Italian is decent enough to know Alessio called him "my love." Is this just another overly affectionate Italian thing? I can swear there is some sexual tension between the two of them. In fact, I'm certain of it. It's the most intriguing thing to watch.

Alessio is openly flirting with Dante, and instead of doing anything, Dante is just watching him with that pained expression on his face, squirming uncomfortably in his seat. *What happened 25 years ago?*

I can't imagine Dante as a 19-year-old. And I definitely can't imagine him with another guy. Yet, there is something between them and I am eager to find out what. Now that the threat of death seems more like a false alarm, my brain is working overtime to solve the intricate mystery that is Dante and Alessio's relationship.

"We should continue this conversation somewhere more...comfortable. How about a drink in my penthouse? It's only one floor up," Alessio suggests, and I'm eager to accept. The view must be next level up there!

Besides, it's not like there's any point trying to get downstairs again. Judging by the CCTV feed, we've missed most of the show already. I don't even have FOMO about that; I'm too curious about Alessio and his connection to Dante. I'm not ready to let this mystery go unsolved.

It doesn't take much to rationalize the decision in my mind. This is obviously not the day I start being a less impulsive person. *Fuck that; it sounds boring.*

But it's not entirely up to me. "We should leave," Dante finally speaks up, albeit not very loudly. He's twisting his rings as he watches Alessio intently. I know his mind is far away when he does that. I just wish I had a ticket for the show behind his eyelids. But not today.

Alessio lowers his voice, his tone deep and serious. "You're in the enemy's lair now, *amore mio.* Your time for leaving has passed. If I were you, I'd do as instructed. I could always call my guards in again." It's a somewhat playful warning, but a warning nonetheless.

"We mean you no harm," I quickly say, almost stammering over my words.

"It's too early for me to say the same." Alessio grins, the hint of a threat smoothed over by his playful tone. "For you at least. For this magnificent beast, I mean *a lot* of harm." He buries his hand in Dante's hair, tightening his fingers as he pulls, forcing my gloomy Don to face him—and Dante lets him, offering no resistance, just a scowl.

There's an air of playful danger that makes it impossible for me to read the situation.

"Do what you want with me, but don't you dare lay a finger on her," Dante hisses as Alessio wraps his fingers around Dante's thick neck, not squeezing, just holding him in a move that appears intimidating yet intimate.

"Do what I want to you? Hmm...Be careful what you wish for, Don Fera. For now, let's go!" Alessio releases Dante and extends his hand to me, pulling me from the chair in a single swoop.

Moving too quickly, I trip on the carpet and come inches from hitting my head on the desk. Luckily Alessio catches me in time, pulling me against him with a firm grip.

Before releasing me, he dips me backward like we're dancing some fancy dance, and I can't help but laugh at the silliness, giggling almost. It's impossible to remain scared of the mysterious Vegas man. He smells nice.

Alessio weaves his fingers through mine, leading me to the door like a gentleman. We both look back at Dante who appears glued to his seat, unmoving. I want to drop Alessio's hand, to go back for Dante, but the Joker holds me in his grip firmly.

"Better come with, Don Fera, or who knows what I might do to this pretty little thing. I mean, just look at that body." Alessio drops his hand to my waist, and a flutter of lust stirs in my belly.

Jesus, Danica. Snap out of it. Stop crushing on the bad guy. Though, calling Alessio the bad guy seems a bit extreme. He has kind eyes...

Focus, Danica! He could still be dangerous.

But Dante doesn't seem worried about safety; he's worried about something different all together—I can see it written all over his face as he finally gets up.

"This is a terrible idea," Dante mutters, begrudgingly following us out the door.

Alessio's arm remains around me, resting comfortably on my waist, as he escorts me past his guards. He is just a bit shorter than Dante, a bit leaner, but he is still way bigger than me. *Maybe they went to school together?*

Once the elevator doors slide shut behind us, Alessio finally releases my fingers. Quick, before Dante can stop him, our host hooks his fingers into my grumpy tattooed god's belt, pulling him towards us and sandwiching me between their bulky figures.

I'm too short to catch the look they exchange, but the fire passing between their bodies is obvious.

The ride up isn't far, and the door slides opens with a subtle ping before anyone can utter a single word.

While Alessio goes ahead, I pull my darling boy aside, desperate to break through his gloomy exterior. Things happened so quickly after those dickheads stuck their guns in our backs, we haven't had time to reconnect. Alessio really needs to work on his methods; that whole situation was unnecessary.

"You okay, baby?" I whisper, brushing my fingers over his cheek affectionately.

Dante sighs, shoulders slumped like they're too heavy to hold up. "I don't know."

"Are we in danger?"

"No—" he starts but Alessio interrupts him, ushering us inside for a tour. A double-volume atrium rises majestically before us, giving the space an airy, almost ethereal feel.

"Come in, come in," the host insists.

Dante pulls away from me as soon as Alessio walks in, out of reach.

"No need for such seriousness," the Joker declares, snapping his fingers to open the automatic blinds. My jaw drops as the shimmering Vegas appears in all its splendor.

"Holy shit." I gasp, walking over to the window to get a better look, instantly distracted.

The 180-degree floor-to-ceiling windows dominate the far wall, offering an uninterrupted view of the glittering Las Vegas skyline. It's a sea of lights, twinkling like a thousand stars against the inky night sky. I'm instantly charmed.

I feel like I'm floating above the city, looking out over a kingdom of neon and dreams. The dark hues of the room's decor—deep charcoals, sleek blacks, and rich, dark woods—create a striking contrast against the vibrant cityscape beyond the glass. It's minimalist yet impossibly elegant, each piece of furniture carefully chosen to complement the overall aesthetic.

"A tour, m'lady?" Alessio offers, and I gladly accept, allowing him to steer me around like we're on some home improvement reality show. Except you'd be hard-pressed to find a way to improve this place. It's perfect!

Dante stays behind as Alessio leads me around for our brief yet breathtaking tour. I'm hoping the alone-time will do him good, help him get his thoughts in order, but it can go either way. You never know with Dante. I might as well enjoy the tour.

The large suite is super modern, a refreshing change from all the old mansions Dante has been taking me to. Fancy furniture, lots of plants, and art that is probably very expensive—it is a comfortable space filled with all the luxurious things rich people have in their apartment: lights that come on when you snap your fingers; wine that costs more than my tuition...

To my left, the open-plan living area sprawls invitingly. A sectional sofa, upholstered in soft black leather, wraps around a low coffee table made of some wood I don't know the name of. On my right, the sleek, modern kitchen stretches out, while on my right, a floating staircase with glass balustrades spirals upwards.

Upstairs, the luxury continues. He doesn't show me what is behind all the doors but the master bedroom opens up to its own portion of the expansive windows, offering a private slice of that breathtaking view.

The king-sized bed, draped in crisp, white linens, stands out against the dark walls, painted some shade of green that is darker than a Christmas tree. Across from it, a huge mirror breaks up the Vegas skyline with a different view—us. I've never seen anything like it, just panes of clear glass mixed with strategically placed mirror panes.

It's a lot to take in, and I can't help but feel a sense of awe at the sheer splendor of it all. Imagine living in a place like this, waking up with a view like that? *Wow*.

Even after being with Dante for a year, spoiled with a virtually limitless credit card and permission to have whatever I want, a year of fancy gala events and even fancier weddings, I am still taken by the grandeur of the lives that men like Alessio and Dante lead. A fortune acquired through nefarious means still buys the same things as any other fortune.

"Should we have some wine?" Alessio offers once our short tour concludes, gently touching my waist to guide me. There is more to see but we both seem eager to get back downstairs, to where Dante is yet to move, so I nod, accepting Alessio's offer.

The host waltzes off to the kitchen, as I check in with the gloomy Don downstairs.

"Baby..." I start, and Dante sighs, leaning back against the door, pulling away from me.

What is up with him?

****UNSENT LETTER #3

The second time you kissed me was after that sleepless night of torment where I repeated the image of your lips on mine until it faded like a worn snapshot.

This time I was the one corrupting you, tempting you to sneak away again, luring you back to the safety of the dark clubs around us.

I had more emotions than words. You told me not to bother trying to make sense of it. I told you it was wrong. You told me "wrong" was subjective. I continued listing reasons why not as your tongue slid over my neck and nipped at my earlobe, turning every protest into an uncontrollable gasp of desire.

Do you want me to stop? you asked, my face in your hands, your body pressed against mine in the middle of the crowd dancing around us as we stood still, kissing, groping, yearning.

Please don't, I begged, pulling you closer to me. I couldn't get enough of you, I wanted it all, as much as that scared me.

I wanted to give you the entire world, and not just for lust. For the way you looked at me with affection in those playful eyes, the way you listened to me (really listened), the way you kissed my wrists tenderly.

Please let's stay here forever. Please.

But we both knew we were on borrowed time.

CHAPTER NINE

HOST

DANICA...

R ather ungracefully, I plonk down on the fancy leather couch to find it as comfortable as it looks. The thought of stretching out on it, shoes and all, is rather tempting—it's big enough to fit two of me. But I resist, bringing my attention back to Dante, who is still hovering by the door.

"Come here, baby," I call him over, patting the seat next to me in invitation.

With a grumble of words that I don't catch, Dante begrudgingly does as he's told, sitting down on the edge of the couch, almost like he's afraid to touch it.

Trying to find his gaze, I take his hand in mine, kissing it sweetly. "You're acting very strange. Should I be worried?" Caressing his cheek, I steer his eyes to mine. There's so much he's not telling me.

Dante sighs. "Probably."

"About Alessio?" I ask quickly.

"No, Alessio won't harm us..."

That's all I need to know. I can't imagine Alessio harming anyone, but if Dante has taught me anything, it's that looks can be deceiving. Who knows what Alessio is really like? All I have to go off is vibes, but dear lord, the vibes are all tingly and sexual.

"I wish you would tell me how you know him." I sigh, knowing it's no use to push. Dante's brain shuts down like this sometimes—when he's overwhelmed—I've learned that by now. All he needs is time, and maybe more alcohol.

"I know." Dante doesn't elaborate.

I squeeze his hand and he returns the gesture. "I'll tell you; I promise I will. I just—" he's cut off by Alessio placing three beautiful crystal glasses on the table in front of us.

I want to hear more but the moment has passed. As soon as Alessio walks in, Dante freezes over again like hell on a bad day (or maybe it's a *good* day). Who knows?

For now, it's wine time, and I, for one, am relieved by the distraction, something to do with my hands.

The long-haired Joker that is Alessio seamlessly pulls the cork on a bottle adorned with dates and writing that would probably impress a more cultured person but mean nothing to me. It all tastes the same. (I've been known to put my red wine in the fridge, a habit that Dante quickly forced out of me.)

"A toast!" Alessio declares, lifting his glass and swirling the dark red liquid inside.

Glass in hand, I get up and tug on Dante's arm to do the same. Like this isn't a totally weird setup, I clink the crystal with those around me, making sure to look both men in the eye during the cheers like my mother taught me. I don't want seven years of bad sex because I didn't make eye contact during a toast. Nobody wants that.

It's a nice wine. I take a big gulp, enjoying the warmth as it trickles down to my stomach, and then another. I should probably slow down, but I appear to be the only one having thoughts of restraint. Dante finishes his glass in one go, putting it down on the table loudly, almost cracking the glass.

"How about some party favors?" Alessio offers, playing his finger over the rim of his glass seductively.

"What does that mean?" I ask as Dante shakes his head in a resounding no.

"Drugs," Dante explains. "We'll pass."

"Not even a little bit of coke like we used to? Maybe some ecstasy? I have everything you could want and more," Alessio boasts.

"I'm good with wine," I reply with a smile. Drugs have never been my thing. A joint here and there, but the chemicals generally don't work well with my brain in my experience.

"Suit yourselves then." Alessio smiles, filling our wine glasses.

He looks at Dante with an intensity that could ignite a dying star, a gaze that is returned with a fire just as bright, before Dante quickly looks away, to the floor. So many glances, so few words.

I watch them intently, the tension between them virtually palpable. *It's hot as fuck*, I decide, as Alessio licks his lips. I've read enough of those MLM romance novels to be completely into whatever sexual dance is unfolding between these tall men.

More than anything, I am intrigued. I've never seen this side of Dante, and I want to know all sides of him intimately. Especially the sides that are reacting to our enigmatic host like they share more than just tattoos.

The whole thing seems so bizarre—like we're in a movie. I'm still not any closer to the answers I seek. But at least the wine is relaxing me a bit.

What happened here all those years back? Were they actually a thing? I know there are a zillion desperate women in Dante's sexual past, but another mafia dude? That's news to me.

"So, can someone tell me what's going on already?" I try my luck, hoping Alessio is feeling more generous with his history lesson. But it's no use.

"We just have some loose ends to tie up, that's all," Alessio answers cryptically, still no straight answers for my questioning mind. "Care to dance?" He finally looks away from Dante and grabs my hand, twirling me around.

"But there's no music?" I laugh, enjoying being spun around like I'm weightless, the wine softening the edges of my anxiety just a bit.

"Alexa, play *Fuego En El Fuego*!" Alessio calls to his home entertainment system and an Italian song with a nice fast beat fills the air at the perfect volume. He pulls me to his chest and dances me around the room in elegant movements that make me feel like I'm gliding, feet barely touching the floor.

He smells so good; it's easy to get lost in the moment in his strong, supportive arms. Dante never cares much for dancing despite my constant attempts to get him to let loose a bit. I had forgotten how much I enjoyed it.

"You're avoiding the question," I insist as Alessio swings me around the room, narrowly avoiding a collision with the life-size statue of some goddess without arms. "Who *are* you?" I try again.

His long, dark hair cascades over his shoulders as we dance, framing a face that could only belong to an angel or a devil—perhaps both. His amber eyes, smokey and mysterious, seem to see right through me, reading every thought I've ever had.

Our host grins. "I'm Alessio and I come in peace."

"You mean us no harm, right?"

"None whatsoever. Unfortunately, I can't say the same for the rest of my family."

"But why?"

"It's not my story to tell, *cara mia*," Alessio says simply, tightening his grip on my hips as he pulls me to my tippy toes, swinging me around until my skirt fans out around me.

This is Dante's queue to jump in and he does, but not with the answers I want. He's way more pissed than I thought.

"Enough!" Dante declares, his voice thundering above the music as he grabs my arm and pulls me away from Alessio like I'm some insolent child. *Fucking hell.* I hate it when he's so aggressive instead of just talking about his feelings like a person.

"Jesus, Dante, I'm just having some fun." Instinctively, I reach toward him, but he pushes me aside, gently but assertively.

"We shouldn't be here," Dante says simply as something foreign flashes in his eyes, a look I've never seen. But he's not looking at me, he's staring daggers at Alessio as his fists clench and unclench by his side like a toddler throwing a tantrum.

I want to hug my darling boy, to make sure he's okay, but Alessio gets to him first, grabbing a momentarily unclenched fist into his hands and pulling Dante toward him while declaring, "Let's dance, darling."

Oh god, this isn't going to end well.

CHAPTER TEN

NOSTALGIA

DANTE...

Alessio grabs my hand, and instantly, I'm back at the club, 25 years ago. The past meshes with the present as he pulls me to him with a firm grip, steering me across the makeshift dance floor of his penthouse apartment with Vegas as our backdrop—again.

Just like then, I'm on a knife's edge, breath imprisoned in my throat, as I let Alessio lead me. The last time he slipped his arm around my waist like this, they were pumping techno through the club's speakers as we slow danced in the shadows, surrounded by unfamiliar bodies; lost in a crowd—just Alessio and I. Young, horny, confused...

But Alessio of the past dissipates as flesh-and-blood Alessio gently lifts my chin to lure my eyes to his. Just for a second. But a second is enough. I know he feels it too. But—

Before I can speak, before I can do anything, Alessio spins me away from him so fast, I almost lose my footing. But he doesn't let go.

Even though I should pull myself together, I can't. I'm lost in those playful amber eyes that promised me the world a quarter of a century ago. A world I wanted, despite everything, despite knowing I shouldn't.

Blood rushes to my head as he dips me like I'm the girl. *How can he do that?* Nobody can do that. I'm too big.

But Alessio is strong—he's not the lanky boy he used to be—and he pulls me up with momentum that sends me crashing into his lean bulk so fast that we almost knock over a coffee table.

It's too much. I can't breathe. I'm overly aware of myself and my body, of Danica standing a few feet apart, watching us intently, all of Vegas beyond the glass. *This is wrong!*

"No," I mutter, digging my feet into the ground and pulling away.

But Alessio isn't letting go that easily.

"We should leave," I insist, pulling my arm from Alessio's iron grip and breaking the spell. Instantly, I miss the contact. I shouldn't, but I do. *What the fuck, Dante?*

"Nonsense, the night has just begun!" Alessio exclaims, winking at Danica as she tops up her glass with more wine. *Jesus.* We don't need more alcohol. This has already gone too far.

Fucking Alessio. Now? Here? I haven't thought about him in years. No, that's a lie. I've been thinking of him non-stop since I saw that Vegas skyline, but it's more than that. He comes back to me more often than I'll ever confess to. Even after all those years, the Alessio-shaped hole in my heart never closed, never scarred over completely.

No matter how much I want this, I am ill at ease; I can't just spontaneously throw myself into a situation the way Danica does. The danger is still very real, and keeping Danica safe is my first priority. I don't know what game Alessio is playing, but the Feras and Santoros haven't been friends in a long time. How can I trust this man who should feel like a stranger but doesn't?

Alessio tries to spin me again, but this time, I'm prepared, stubbornly digging my heels into the floor. "I don't dance, Alessio," I say simply.

He sighs dramatically. "Aww, don't be such a spoilsport, *amore mio.*"

"I'm nothing of yours," I hiss through gritted teeth as feelings churn my insides in knots, feelings I can't describe. The only one that feels familiar, that feels comfortable enough to pluck from the muddled mess, is anger. I know what to do with anger.

But I'm not the only one with feelings.

As I turn to walk away, Alessio slams my body into the wall with his, hard enough to make me see stars. He presses his face right up against mine, so close our noses are virtually touching. We're both breathing too fast; I can feel his chest heaving up and down with mine.

Alessio's voice is an angry whisper that only I can hear. "Nothing? Tell me again, dear Dante, tell me how we were *nothing*."

I hesitate for only a second and that's all he needs. Alessio closes the short distance between us and forces my lips open with his tongue. Like I've dreamt of more nights than I'll ever confess to anyone (especially myself), he kisses me roughly, messily, his tongue sliding against mine as he steals what little air I held back in my lungs. Instinctively, I kiss him back; I don't want to, but I do; my body knows I do.

Dio mio. I've wanted this for eternity—25 years of unreleased desire that flares up in an instant like we are back at that club, hesitant hands touching, hearts racing...like the first time he kissed me. *Fuck!*

The panic pushes up in my throat. I push Alessio off me before I drown in him, in the moment.

He staggers back but keeps his footing, that sly smirk still parked on his face.

"That ship has sailed," I say. It takes everything I have to keep my eyes glued on his as he searches my expression for the truth I know I'm not hiding very well.

But it's not just my eyes that betray me.

Alessio closes the distance again and presses his hips against mine, his unmistakable erection outlined against my own. "Really? That ship has sailed? Then why are you so hard for me, *amore mio*?" He grinds his hips slowly, rubbing his hardness against mine.

That's when I freak out. I don't mean to, but I do. The moment is too big, the emotion too much.

So, I do the only thing I know to do when I feel threatened: I punch him—square in the jaw. *Fuck.*

Alessio immediately backs off, raising a hand to his bruising cheek.

Part of me wants to throw another right hook, to ruin that handsome face, but Danica's voice halts me. I stop, fist mid-air.

"Dante *Fucking* Fera!" she shouts, inventing a middle name for me like I'm some naughty child in big trouble. "Stop!"

Alessio ducks to avoid the punch that doesn't come.

"Don't hit him. Jesus. You're being ridiculous," Danica scolds, making me feel like I'm ten years old again.

I'm no longer looking at Alessio, I've been pulled into the orb of my Goddess, my Queen, and I instantly feel ashamed of my actions. I look down, hands trembling.

"I'm sorry," I sulk, barely audible. I shouldn't have punched him. Danica doesn't like violence, especially not what she calls "unnecessary violence," which I'm sure this qualifies as. This is the opposite of me using my words. But my brain isn't working as it should today. Everything is upside down.

"Look at me," Danica instructs, and I meet her gaze, embarrassed—not just for the punch but for everything. "You're behaving like a bad boy again, aren't you?" Her voice is thick with a patronizingly sweet reprimand. My cheeks flush.

"I'm sorry," I say softly, my shoulders hunched in shame. I want to add "Miss" but I'm overly aware of Alessio's presence.

"I'm not the one you owe an apology."

I offer a "Sorry" to Alessio, but I know it's not sufficient. He nods, leaving it at that, though.

"Are you going to behave yourself already?" Danica asks, clearly annoyed.

"I promise."

Her expression softens to affection and she takes my hand. "Be good, okay?"

I nod, trying to pull myself together. The last thing I want is to do any damage to my relationship with Danica. She comes first, always—even if my stupid cock Sonja has a mind of its own today, running after old fantasies.

"More wine, anyone?" Alessio breaks the tension, gently putting a hand on Danica's shoulder.

I don't think more wine is going to help my judgment...but I nod either way, avoiding his eyes as I hope he doesn't notice my flushed cheeks burning with humiliation. Nothing quite like having your partner reprimand you for punching your teenage crush in the face.

What the fuck, though?

The entire situation still feels like some weird dream but my almost painful erection reminds me that it's very real.

Fucking Sonja.

**UNSENT LETTER #4

After the second sleepless night replaying the taste of your lips, there was no sneaking away again. I wanted to so badly, I wanted you, all of you. But instead, all I got was an order to leave the city immediately.

Friendly rivals had turned into sworn enemies in our absence; we couldn't stay in Vegas. I argued and pleaded but the family's mind was set—it was war. And you were now my enemy. Why couldn't I see you as such? Why couldn't I see you as anything other than the one person I finally wanted to sacrifice my purity for? I wanted you to take me, to break me, to make me feel something, anything other than this monotony.

We could run away. We could start afresh, away from all this responsibility, my destiny. We could go somewhere they'd let us be together, let us have our fun. I would pick up the guitar again like when my mother was alive. You could learn to surf or work on your poems. We could be happy.

But family first, my father said, watching as they carried our luggage from the lobby.

Family first.

CHAPTER ELEVEN

GASPING

DANICA...

A lessio opens another bottle of red as he turns the music up, blaring a mix of sensual yet rhythmic Italian songs from the overhead speakers. Dante doesn't say much. He just sits back on the couch and nurses his drink.

My darling Don seems lost in thought but watches us intently, watches as Alessio takes my hand and resumes our dance, watches as the Joker pulls me closer and closer until he fills my entire world.

The wine is warm inside me, making everything feel easier, like I'm floating from one scene to the next. I'm not drunk, but I'm jovial nonetheless, free.

My rational mind knows I should probably be weary of the stranger steering me around so effortlessly, but I'm too absorbed by Alessio's magnetic energy to give a fuck.

What is it about this city that makes you feel like you can, and should, do anything? A world without consequences, just shiny lights and platters and platters of temptation. I should've come here sooner.

Alessio lures my full attention back to him as he crosses his wrists behind the small of my back, resting his hands comfortably against my ass. "I want to kiss you, *bella mia*," he whispers, amber gaze imploring me to just give in. Alessio looks at me with such intensity, those gorgeous lips so close, that I'm convinced my heart has stopped doing its work. *Oh god.*

"Then do it," I dare him.

I don't think he'll actually do it. Still, part of me wants him to—really badly. Especially because I know Dante is watching. He's watched me kiss another before. Granted, it was Adira. But still, he's watched and so have I...But this is different.

I look past Alessio to my darling boy who is still lost in his inner world. Dante can hear everything we're saying from his sulking position on the couch, nursing his drink. But he doesn't interject.

Alessio spins me around so he can face Dante as he speaks. "I'm afraid your boyfriend will punch me again," he says.

"I won't punch you," Dante says simply. I can't see the look he gives Alessio, if any. But the way Alessio grins, I'm sure Dante reacted.

Looking back, I search my grumpy love's face, trying to read his deadpan expression. I'm torn between wanting to comfort him and being irresistibly drawn to Alessio. Either way, I don't want to hurt Dante. "Does that mean you approve of me kissing him?" I ask.

Our contract has "cuckolding" on Dante's green list, so I know I'm not straying too far out of bounds. We've talked about it before but haven't found the right play partner yet. Still, I could never do anything without his consent. Never.

"I didn't say I approve, just that I won't punch him." Dante's tone is indecipherable, neutral verging on cold.

"Are you jealous?" I know he gets jealous easily, the same as me. He once almost punched his own brother because he thought the asshole was hitting on me (which he was).

"Yes and no." Dante doesn't bother to clarify; he just takes another sip of his drink.

I want to ask a follow-up question but Alessio is done talking.

"Good enough," Alessio declares and pulls me in for a kiss so soft yet passionate...delicately intimate. His lips lightly brush mine, arms wrapped around me tightly as he dips me back just a little like we're in some rom-com movie.

"Hmm," I mutter, opening my eyes when he finally lets me go.

Alessio flicks his tongue over my lips like I'm made of candy. "You taste delicious."

"Um, you too?" *Is this what I'm supposed to say? Oh god, I sound dumb.*

"You lucky, lucky boy, Dante." Alessio smiles over my shoulder.

Dante just grunts, watching us closely. I still don't know if he's mad or into it, but he's not rushing over to punch Alessio, so that's a start.

"Let's do that again," Alessio proposes, twirling me around in his arms like we're still dancing, even though we've stopped.

Dante gets up from the couch to open another bottle of wine. He's right beside us as Alessio deepens our second kiss, his long fingers exploring the curve of my breasts over my dress. My breath catches in my throat as Alessio pulls my body into his, touching me, groping me, devouring my lips in a frenzy I did not expect.

When we finally part, gasping for air, Dante is standing frozen before us, wine overflowing from the glass onto the expensive-looking carpet that someone else will have to clean.

"Did you enjoy the show, darling?" Alessio asks, hooking a finger into a belt loop in Dante's pants and pulling the mute tattoo god toward us. One hand still resting against my ass, Alessio reaches over to Dante's cock, tracing its outline against the fabric with a single finger in an incredibly intimate move.

Dante gasps at the unexpected gesture, his tight pants straining even tighter as his hardness grows. He doesn't move though; he stands frozen between us, his breathing loud and rapid.

My darling boy is not scared; he's nervous. He'd look different if this was a life-or-death situation rather than a Dante's-brain-short-circuiting situation. I know him well enough to know that. Nervous and hard as fuck, clearly.

I have an idea. Despite knowing it's a ridiculous one, I also don't care...

I want to see it, I *long* to see it, I *need* to see it.

"Do you want to suck him off?" I ask softly, placing my hand over Alessio's and guiding it over Dante's pants to stroke his erection together.

Dante grunts like a wild animal, eyes wide as his body stiffens under our touch.

Our host speaks before Dante can muster an answer. "You wouldn't mind sharing?" he asks me.

"Not at all. I would love to watch," I reassure him.

Dante groans in response, breathing in rapid little breaths as he looks from me to Alessio, and then back. The torment of indecision strains his expression into a pained look.

"While he decides..." Alessio grins, pulling me in for another hungry kiss as we rub Dante to full hardness, together.

I return my attention to Dante. "What do you say, *Tesoro*? Will you boys put on a show for me? I would love to touch myself while I watch..." This has long been a fantasy of mine, though I never thought Dante would be up for such a thing. Clearly, I have much to learn about him.

As much as I know it won't make thinking any easier, I reach for Dante's belt, slowly unzipping his pants so I can lift his erection from the restrictive confines of the material holding it. "There you are," I smile, my fingers wrapped around his dick, stroking him under the tip of his head, just how he likes it.

Dante squirms under my touch, panting softly. I know how he loves my dirty talk. But we've never done it in front of another man before. He doesn't stop me though; he doesn't push me away. No, he melts in my hand.

If he really wanted to leave, he'd chuck me over his shoulder and drag me out of here—I wouldn't be able to stop him. But he doesn't want to leave...

My heart pounds, a shiver of desire rushing through me like a fever. I'm overly aware of Alessio's proximity, his smell, his watchful amber gaze that seems to drip with temptation.

Dante isn't the only one who likes to perform, to be watched. "Feel me," I breathe as I hike my skirt up over my hips and guide Dante's hand down my panties to the wetness pooling between my thighs. "Do you feel how wet I am, baby?"

Dante nods, hypnotized. He doesn't dare move as I grind my hips against his hand, coating his fingers in my need. Maybe now he'll get the picture; see just how fucking turned on I am by all this.

"Do you want to taste?"

Without breaking our gaze, Dante nods and brings his fingers to his lips, sucking me off his digits slowly, stoking the desire flaring up in my belly.

"You make me so happy when you're being a good boy," I tell him as I reach up to kiss him, enjoying the taste of my lust on his lips. I press my body against Dante's, trapping his hard cock between us as I whisper, "Do you want this, darling?"

Dante nods slowly, casting his eyes to the floor. He shuffles from one foot to the other, shoulders slumped.

I tip his chin to me, forcing his eyes back on mine. "Look at me, baby. Say your words. Do you want this?"

Dante exhales loudly. "I do," he confirms his consent. His voice is small, soft—nothing like the confident tone the tattooed god uses to command his army. It melts my heart every time.

"I love you no matter what." I squeeze his hand.

"I love you too," Dante replies, placing my hand over his heart. A simple move but one that lets me know he's okay.

"Now don't you fucking dare come without permission!" My tone changes as I smack Dante's sensitive erection with the back of my hand, sending him doubling over in agony.

By now, it should be very clear to Alessio who holds the power in this dynamic, but he doesn't comment on it. I doubt someone who runs a place like this would be very conservative. Besides, Alessio doesn't seem to care much for traditional gender norms judging by the hint of eyeliner that smudges under his eyes. Well, that, and his entire fluid vibe.

"He's all yours, Alessio. Just make sure I get a good view." Tugging at the neck of his open shirt, I reach up for a sloppy kiss from our host, brushing my tongue against his to make sure he gets a taste of my lust too. *Just a taste.*

"I want more of that later," Alessio promises, caressing my ass as I break away.

My panties slide onto the floor before dropping onto the large L-shaped black leather couch in the middle of the room. Legs open wide, I hike my skirt up around my waist, my bottom half fully unclothed for easy access. I meant what I said to the men—I have every intention of *watching*.

And that's what I do. I watch as the beautiful Italian god with the shampoo-commercial hair gets on his knees before Dante, *my* Dante.

Despite worrying that I might, I don't feel uncomfortable or awkward or like a third wheel as I watch Dante groan softly, and then louder. I feel empowered! Hungry. Lustful. Christ, I am hornier than I've ever been.

But most of all, I feel excited for Dante. I didn't expect it, but watching Dante's face contort with a million feelings he could never voice as Alessio takes his length inside his mouth...in this moment, I feel no jealousy, only love.

Eyes on the scene, I hum softly, letting my fingers slip down over my clit...

CHAPTER TWELVE

DESPERATE

DANTE...

Alessio drops to his knees and life switches to dream mode, unfolding in slow motion.

I don't stop him—I don't want to.

Last time, *I* was the one on my knees, not him. Last time...when they caught us, when Alessio got taken away. *Fuck.* I still can't think of that day without the shame dragging me down like a dead weight.

All these years, I thought it was too late for a do-over. Yet here he is, Prince Santoro himself, as beautiful as ever (especially from this vantage point), pulling my pants down to beneath my ass.

My core clenches to the point of muscle spasm as I try to hold everything together; to not come undone immediately as Alessio caresses my cock like he's stroking a pet.

As much as I want to close my eyes, I don't want to look away either; I want to see everything. I still can't process the fact that it's him, really him.

Age has been kind to my childhood best friend; he's grown into the sharp facial features that made him look so eccentric as a teenager.

I want him as much now as I wanted him then—I know that for a fact as he closes his lips around the tip of my cock.

A desperate moan escapes my lips and I don't try and stop it; I don't try and stop any of it. I have Danica's blessing, even if I don't 100% have my own.

My body wants this, wants this so badly that it burns through my flesh like a disease. I would tear off my skin and throw it on the floor just to stop this feeling, this insatiable aching for him that consumes me now as much as it did back then. There is no denying that my body wants this.

But my mind is a different story. My mind has lived through 45 years of training to be the alpha male, the boy who doesn't cry, the man who kills without emotion. My mind cannot accept this need: it's desperately fighting my body with every inch of my cock Alessio swallows deeper and deeper until he has my entire length between those sensual lips.

You're a fucking pussy, grow up, Dante! I still hear my father's voice back then, after they caught us in the shadowy club that failed to hide our awkward exploration of desire.

The memory replays in my mind as Alessio slides my pants all the way down to my ankles. I kick it off along with my underwear, exposing my ass to the Vegas skyline, to the city stretching out beyond the large glass windows with the blinds still open all the way.

Your family depends on you, my father's voice refuses to shut up, adding more traffic to my already buzzing circuits. *It doesn't matter what your dick wants.*

Still, I moan even louder as Alessio spits me out and devours me all over again, his hand wrapped around my balls, cupping them, tugging gently like he knows how crazy that drives me.

This life is not yours to waste, son. You're a Fera—act like one.

I didn't listen then and I don't listen now. No, I grab a fistful of Alessio's long hair and pull as hard as I can, grinding my cock into his mouth with an unsuppressed lustful growl.

Enough!

There is only so much any man can resist. And my resistance is officially shot; I'm done.

My eyes drift to Danica on the couch, not even three yards away. I don't even have to wonder if she's okay;

she clearly is. My Queen blows me a kiss as she moans loudly for our pleasure as much as hers, speeding up the movement as she fingers herself. I could never tire of seeing her face wrenched in pleasure.

What a crazy wild child Danica is. How is she okay with watching this? But of course, she is. Things that torment me, she accepts without question.

We share a secret smile before I shift my gaze back to the handsome villain on the floor, my cock throbbing in his mouth. Despite the many, many scenarios that have run through my head since we arrived on the forbidden runway, none of them included anything remotely like this.

I thought I would find Francesco here, not Alessio...

But now's not the time to dwell on the past, not with every nerve-ending exploding in desire.

With those liquid pools of amber ablaze with lust, Alessio looks up at me as he takes in all of me—virtually choking on my cock. He keeps my gaze boldly as I fuck his face, again and again until my pre-cum moistens his lips.

I want it all, I want to finish. "Please!" I howl, gasping.

"Don't you dare," Danica hisses from the side. She knows me so well. "I said no coming." She moves quickly, pulling Alessio off my cock before I can finish...kissing him first and then me.

Instantly, I miss Alessio's lips around my dick.

What the fuck am I doing?

We're all panting, all for different yet similar reasons, all so close to the edge.

"I'm bursting," I confess in our kiss, holding Danica tight as I try to regain my senses.

"I know you are, baby. But rules are rules. Down, Sonja." She flicks a finger at my hard cock, just enough to be painful, disrupting the desperate loop in my mind and forcing me to the present.

Despite the pain, I smile faintly at Danica, grateful that she's here to share this moment with me, to ground me. I feel lost and found at the same time. But it's not just about *my* needs...

Alessio joins us, seductively running his hand over the curve of Danica's hip as he winks at me. "Hmm...It would appear I haven't sampled *all* the items on the menu yet."

Danica grins mischievously at him and then looks at me. "You want to watch?"

Another one I did not have on my bingo card: Danica and Alessio.

I did not see this coming.

Yet I'm not surprised, not in the slightest.

Fuck it. Who am I to deny her pleasure?

So, I nod—yes. There's no point questioning *why* at this stage. The mere thought of Danica and Alessio together like this is so incredibly arousing!

Danica kisses me deeply and then returns her focus to Alessio. I know she likes leaving me on the edge—dripping and needy. It doesn't make my pesky erection any less uncomfortable though.

But I would never dare do anything about it, not without permission.

Instead, I sink onto the couch where Danica sat earlier, playing with herself as she watched Alessio suck me off. She didn't finish though; she didn't come...I would've heard if she did; Danica is so loud usually. *What is she up to?*

From the couch, I see the unlikely pair exchange inaudible whispers. Danica laughs nervously but nods in agreement as Alessio starts undressing himself, slowly discarding his layers in a sensual strip show meant for me as much as for Danica.

The way he looks at me, the grin he sends my way as he slides his pants down—I don't feel neglected at all.

It's hard to think about anything other than my own desperate need to come; my hardness aches as Alessio's stunning cock finally springs free—thick, ready. He stands proud, watching me watch him as I bask in his nakedness.

Even at 43, his body is hard and muscular, but in a lean way—like a swimmer.

I remain frozen on the couch, watching intently as Alessio leads Danica to the full-size day bed by the window.

There's a moment of slight awkwardness as they figure out who's in charge and what next, but only a moment.

Then Danica grins devilishly and pushes Alessio down on the large seat nearly the size of a double bed, stalking over him like a cheetah. He lets her.

My erection is aching but I know I can't do anything about it. I want to touch myself as Danica swallows Alessio's cock, licking him up and down with those perfectly non-smeared red lips of hers. But Mistress said no touching, so I don't.

Alessio holds my gaze for as long as he can, closing his eyes when the pleasure becomes too much. Danica is good at what she does, I can tell on Alessio's face that I'm not the only one who thinks so. I want to be him *and* fuck him at the same time!

There are too many emotions crowding my mind. Part of it is jealousy; possessiveness over Danica. She is mine and I don't want to share her. As much as I have cuckolding fantasies, I've never been able to actually pursue them. I don't want to risk losing her. *What if she wants Alessio instead of me?*

But another part of me, a larger part, feels pure lust. Watching Danica perform, watching her so confident, so sure of herself, of her body. *Oh god, I want her more than ever.* Right now, in this moment, I am so proud of her for taking what she wants.

A third part of me, the part I don't want to think about, is jealous of Danica's hands on Alessio, of anyone laying their hands on him, on *my* Alessio.

But he was never mine, they made sure of it.

I study Alessio's expression in detail as Danica brings him to orgasm, watch the glow of bliss on his face, that carefree wonder, the twitch in his eye as he gets close. I want to be the one who makes him hum in pleasure like that—I almost was that one time...

But I don't want to dwell on this part. It reminds me that we're still in danger simply by being here, that we have to get out. Alessio's brother is still the head of the family and he's made it *very* clear that he never wants to see my face again. Finding me half-naked in his little brother's penthouse would doubtfully be met with a positive reaction.

But I'm not going anywhere, I'm glued to the show.

Besides, why would Francesco be here? He has no reason to suspect I'm back.

Alessio winks at me as he bites his bottom lip seductively, a loud growl resonating from his lips. "I'm close," he warns her.

"On my tits," Danica demands boldly, pulling away just in time.

Thick cum spurts from Alessio's cock onto her cleavage, only partially reaching its target.

The dramatic release is more breathtaking than any show at a club could ever be—a performance with an audience of one, me.

Alessio falls back on the bed as Danica gets up, inspecting the sticky mess on her outfit. Like I'm in a trance, I walk over to them, closing the short distance between us with my hands clenched at my sides, straining to not touch my cock.

Danica pulls me in as soon as I'm within reach.

"Clean up?" she proposes with a twinkle in her eye as I lean in to kiss her, my tongue exploring the foreign taste on her lips...

"Hmm...Gladly." I lick Alessio from her lips, her collarbone, the groove between her breasts...her neck. I find every drop of him and consume it with a feverishness that burns through me, savoring the taste of passion spent.

"Such a sweetheart. Did you like the performance?" Danica asks when I run out of places to clean and I nod, smiling.

"It was so hot," I admit, kissing her back with my cum-stained lips.

The naked Alessio gets up and joins us, kissing Danica first and then rewarding me with a kiss too. This time I don't push him or punch him. No, I give into the moment, exhaling a sigh of relief as the man who almost ruined me all those years ago lures me into his web again.

His lips are soft, warm, and desperate for mine as his tongue explores my mouth. My cock jumps, still eager to be part of the action.

Oh god, I'm coming undone. Again.

It's just like before.

Except this time, Danica is lost in the spell too.

**UNSENT LETTER #5

I had to go back—I couldn't leave like that, not without speaking to you, my Dark Prince. Was this all one-sided? Was it only me? I had to know, had to know what you wanted.

One last rendezvous in the shadows of the sex club whose name you wrote on a little piece of paper and slipped under my door. One more sneak-away to your warm lips, your comfortable embrace, your hardness pressed against mine in wanting.

This time I didn't stop your wandering hands as they caressed my skin, drawing breathless moans from my body as your fingers played over the strained fabric of my pants. Hesitantly, I allowed my hands to explore you in response, indecision quickly growing to confidence as my need for you intensified. There was too much fabric between us.

The world around me melted in a blur as you led me to a semi-private room, as you pushed me to my knees, freeing *that gorgeous cock from your jeans. I had never touched another one before, never marveled at its beauty (never thought I would). But you gave yourself to me without shame, let yourself be tasted, sucked, enjoyed.*

Neither of us heard them come in; neither of us noticed the familiar faces until it was too late...until they dragged you out of there kicking and screaming, leaving me on my knees with a painfully hard erection and a black eye...alone.

CHAPTER THIRTEEN

DECISIONS

DANTE...

I n the ultimate power move, Danica gives me back my freedom. It freezes me, short-circuiting the fragile wiring in my overstimulated brain.

"It's your choice, baby. How do you want to come?" she repeats, stroking my cheek tenderly as her eyes explore mine for an answer. Her other arm is wrapped around the still naked, hard-again Alessio, holding the three of us together in a close embrace.

I look at Alessio, my heart pounding faster than it should biologically be able to. *I shouldn't want this.* But I do.

My gaze shifts to Danica, searching. I can't believe she is being so supportive, but that's Danica for you—of course, she's understanding. The ultimate self-proclaimed pleasure-Domme, I know she wants me to be wholly satisfied, happy. Even if it is at someone else's touch.

I was so worried she'd question my masculinity for wanting another man, but her brain doesn't work like that. Where I see binary, Danica sees spectrums. She tried to explain once, but the words didn't make sense until now.

"Say it, baby," she encourages me. Having her blessing makes it easier but harder at the same time—part of me wishes she'd choose for me, forbid me from chasing what I want so badly. But Danica just smiles, squeezing my hand reassuringly.

The tension is so thick you could cut it with a blunt knife, so thick I'm nearly choking on it. This is it. There are no more excuses left, only a choice. My father is no longer around to take the blame; if I reject Alessio now, it's my own doing.

Taking a deep breath to try and steady my nerves, I count to ten before facing Alessio.

"Touch me, please," I whisper, so soft, my voice foreign, shaky, but unmistakably clear.

Oh god. I wish I could sink into the floor, disappear entirely. The silence stretches on, each second feeling like a lifetime. My heart is pounding in my chest as I brace myself for rejection, but it never comes. *Why do I feel like such a fucking teenager around him?*

"I've waited decades to hear you say that, *amore mio*." The Dark Prince smiles and pulls me into his arms, his lips finding mine in an unquenchable thirst that I want to spend eternity trying to quench. All I can smell is Aramis and lust—what a beautiful combination.

Alessio kisses me until the pounding in my heart speeds up instead of slowing down, until my palms are sweaty and my cock aches with intolerable hardness. Every hair on my body is standing upright as I give in to the temptation, finally.

I'm overly aware of the fact that Alessio is completely naked and all I have going in terms of clothing on is my vest and some socks.

Alessio's bare skin sets mine on fire with shivers wherever our bodies meet, both hot and cold at the same time. The evidence is unmistakable: he is hard again, and I've never left that state.

I'm not the only one who's noticed.

"Look how beautiful," Danica coos, wrapping a hand around each of our cocks and damn near sending me over the edge instantly. Alessio smiles at me as Danica presses our lengths together, rubbing them with both hands, our erections trapped together between her fingers.

It's the most arousing experience, almost overwhelmingly so. The little seductress bends down and kisses each of our dicks sweetly and Alessio's body shivers against mine.

By the time Danica looks up to kiss our lips, I know I'm mere moments from coming undone.

"Let's go upstairs," Alessio suggests, and we wordlessly follow him up the floating steps to the master bedroom, hand-in-hand, all three of us with Alessio in the middle. Despite not having a free hand, Alessio manages to drag some wine upstairs too, tucked under his armpit.

After one more kiss to each of us, Danica takes the wine and climbs onto the large bed. But not before whispering in my ear the words that instantly drive me mad: "You have permission, baby. Let me see you come."

I groan in response, no words capable of expressing the emotions I feel, the desires that burn through me like lightning. I've had a lifetime of pushing things down, but not tonight. Tonight I want it all! Even if just for tonight...

"Looks like I finally have you all to myself." Alessio smiles, pulling me in for a soft kiss that quickly turns rough. He bites my lip and shoves me against the wall where the large windows end, his hands all over me, tugging at what's left of my clothes, finding skin beneath, pinching, licking, nibbling...His sharp nails dig into my back and I silently beg for him to mark me.

It is more than physical with Alessio...all the words unsaid, the years unshared, have led up to this dance of back and forth, this insatiable craving.

With more strength than I'll ever use on Danica, I push him away, but he doesn't let go. Alessio drags me back by the hips, slamming our aroused bodies together.

Breathless, I lunge at him, banging him into the wall. He takes me with him, never once breaking eye contact.

Play fighting and real kissing, our aggression mixes with a tenderness that feels almost foreign but so familiar at the same time because it's Alessio. All the things I wanted him to do to my body back then...

"We're not kids anymore," I manage to form a complete sentence as Alessio's hands touch me all over, finally tugging my stupid vest over my head and throwing it on the floor.

"No, we're all grown now," he whispers, nibbling on my exposed neck.

With nothing between us now, I shudder in nervous anticipation as I stand before him completely naked. I want to tell him to do whatever he wants with me but there's no need. There is nobody to stop us this time, just Danica's encouraging smiles whenever my eyes drift to hers.

But as soon as Alessio takes my shaft in his palm, my mind goes quiet, handing him the reigns to my desperate body. Without any resistance, I melt in his touch, ready to explode, but Alessio lets go as quickly as he grabs on. *Cazzo!*

I moan in protest, shoving him away just to do something with my hands. My playful rival nearly loses his balance, but he grabs onto me just in time, almost sending us both tumbling to the floor. I manage to keep my balance in our fight of passion, but only just.

"I'm still older than you, stronger," I tell him defiantly, grabbing his wrist.

But as quick as lightning, Alessio twists his arm out of my grip and turns the tables. He forces my right hand behind my back and shoves me face-first into the wall—hard. Pain shoots from my bruised cheek like a ripple outward.

"Fuck you!" I struggle, but he's got me pinned.

"Oh, I will. Don't you worry, darling," Alessio whispers in my neck, his forearm pressing against my throat in a headlock I cannot escape.

He drags me a few paces to the left until we're both facing one of the full-length mirrors nestled between the giant windowpanes.

The hardness of his erection against my ass is undisputed. My own is pressed against the cold surface of the mirror but no less hard.

Alessio pulls back until I see us both in the reflection, see his body wrapped around mine, his free hand drifting over my waist, lower, lower, to my cock. My breath catches and my entire body grows as stiff as my dick.

I don't reply, I can't. When his hand reaches my cock, I instantly feel like I'm about to make a mess. His hand is warm, his touch rough. It takes every ounce of self-control not to release into his grip there and then.

Alessio tightens his hold on my throat and I struggle for breath—it only makes me harder, more desperate.

My eyes dart to the reflected background, to Danica's beautiful cunt on full display between her spread thighs on the bed behind us, watching us intently in the mirror. She blows me a kiss, rubbing her pussy in time with Alessio's movements over my cock.

I mouth "I love you" to her, and she returns the sentiment. Knowing that I don't have to worry about us, that we'll be okay, makes it easier to give in to the moment, to Alessio's commanding touch, to the fire consuming me from the center out as those slender fingers tease and tug and rub me into a frenzy.

Oh, Dio mio! I've wanted this for so long, but now that it is happening it doesn't feel real. So many half-formed thoughts stall in my brain as Alessio grinds his erection against my ass, pushing me into his ready palm.

Jerking me roughly, Alessio quickly works me to a climax, one that has been building since the moment he turned around in that office one floor down, breaking the wall of feelings and memories I'd tried to keep intact for decades.

Need prickles my skin, seeping into my veins as I try to hold on a bit longer. But I know there's no use.

Louder than I intend, I growl like an animal—sounds all I have left in my vocabulary to express my desires.

But I don't need anything more than sounds. Alessio knows.

"Do it," he whispers in my ear, speeding up his movements as I leak pre-cum all over his fingers. The natural lubricant only encourages his strokes, reducing the friction, increasing the speed.

I moan, almost a whimper, as he nibbles my earlobe, chasing his words with a warm breath that spirals me to a point of near eruption.

"Open your eyes," he instructs, and I force myself out of my head to meet his mirrored gaze. Until now, I didn't even notice my eyes had fallen shut.

I catch sight of myself in the mirror, trying to make sense of the image—it doesn't look like me, but I don't know in what way. Later, I'll realize that this is just how my body looks when it dances to Alessio's touch.

"Look at me. Keep looking at me while you come, *amore mio*," the Dark Prince whispers, licking my ear as he keeps my eyes pinned on our reflection.

Alessio shifts his arm around my throat, giving me only a second of reprieve before clamping down on my windpipe again, trapping my gasping breath inside.

The build-up is nearing its crescendo and I'm about to topple over. Behind us, Danica moans loudly; I know she must be close too.

Keeping my eyes on the amber pool in the mirror, I hold on as long as I can, which isn't long at all. With a loud groan that leaves my strained throat in a whimper, I let go.

I can't keep my eyes open as thick cum spurts all over Alessio's hand, over the mirror, my stomach. The orgasm rips through my body—the most satisfying explosion that releases so much more than just spunk.

Leaning back against the lean bulk behind me, I sink into the bliss entirely, wholly, letting the feeling wash over me without trying to fight anymore.

At some point, Alessio eases his chokehold and my burning lungs gasp for air like a drowning man breaching the surface.

I'm lightheaded and my knees are seconds from betraying me; keeping upright has become a real struggle. But Alessio doesn't let me fall. With both arms wrapped around me, he holds me up firmly...all of me pressed against all of him. His rapid heartbeat pulses against my back as he kisses my sweaty neck while I watch in the mirror, watch how tenderly his lips brush against my skin.

Then he turns me around like I'm not a useless ragdoll right now, hugging me close, my sticky body smearing against his, sticking to him.

"You *are* a good boy," Alessio grins, smacking my ass playfully.

This is the part where I insert a witty comeback, but it's not going to happen today. So, I just rest my head on his shoulders, focusing on his skin against mine, the warmth of it all.

He holds me until my legs work again, until I distance our hug just enough to reach his lips, to kiss him, and say the words I can't believe come from my own mouth; the words I've been choking on for hours: "I've missed you too."

Chapter Fourteen

COMPERSION

Danica...

E yes glued on their bodies, I cannot look away as the men fight and kiss and touch and grope, dancing around the room in a fury fueled by testosterone, lust, nostalgia, and a fair amount of alcohol.

My clit is so sensitive to the touch...I trail my fingers over the delicate nerve endings as I enjoy the real-life erotic show unfolding before me. They're standing so close that I can see Dante shudder in the Joker's arms.

A gasp flutters from my lips as Alessio grabs Dante in that chokehold, spreading his fingers over that desperate cock like I've done so many times myself. He's milking Dante like I'm not even here, except I am, and it's the hottest thing I've ever seen in my life (or porn).

Well, second hottest thing. Number one goes to Alessio. I can't believe I just gave our enigmatic host a

157

blowjob while Dante watched. *Oh god, it was such a hot experience!*

Who knew I'd enjoy performing for two Italian gods with Vegas bustling beneath me? Mind you, I should have known. That sounds right up my alley.

Still, I could never have imagined how this night would turn out—not in my wildest fantasies. The Vegas trip I planned did not include finding another play partner on the itinerary. And definitely not me fingering myself to Dante being jerked off by some shampoo-commercial villain with beautiful skin and elegant hands.

People always told me Vegas was wild, but this shit is next level.

When I ask Dante how he wants to come, I already know the answer. I know, and Dante knows; I'm pretty sure Alessio knows too. But I need him to say it—not for me but for himself.

The anguish on Dante's face is painful to watch, as it has been since we arrived in this city of sin and seduction. I want relief for him as much as I would want it for myself. And not just in the physical sense.

This is not about me, I know that now—I cannot give him what Alessio holds. I think I finally understand the meaning of the word compersion. All I want is for Dante to be happy.

Sure, Dante's desire for Alessio surprised me initially. I never thought my brick house of a Don would be open to exploring physical pleasure beyond the female gender. At the same time, it wasn't such a strange thought at all. That man had a lot of love to give, as much as he tried to push that side of himself down.

This new feeling surprises me; I've never felt something like this before. When I really think about it, I'm not worried about losing Dante at all, no, I know he's mine—now more than ever. This is not an either/ or situation; Alessio and I are not mutually exclusive options.

Oh, Dante. I am so proud of my beautiful sub when he finally gives in, when he utters his desperate plea, his confession for Alessio's touch. The tattooed god has never looked more vulnerable than in this moment, and it is the most exquisite thing to behold.

I'm incredibly aroused by the scene. Sure, I want this for Dante, but I want this for me too; I want to watch, to give into my voyeuristic urges.

But they're not the only urges fluttering in my stomach. Alessio has the most intoxicating influence. I am swept away by his mere presence, his playful yet dangerous vibe.

All this time, I never thought we'd actually find a suitable partner, one who could match the passion that burns between Dante and me. But Alessio is in a league of his own, a god among mortals—worthy. I've never met anyone like him.

The details of their history together remain a mystery to me but their connection is undeniable. Whatever happened between Dante and Alessio all those years ago clearly still had a very strong effect on Dante, on both of them.

Yet there is somehow space for my and Dante's dynamic within whatever the two of them have. But it's not just about what they have (or had). The attraction that sparks between me and Alessio is feverish, urgent.

The power dynamics between us all should be more confusing than they are, yet they aren't. There is a natural rhythm that our bodies already know long before our minds can make sense of it.

Between my fingers, my wetness spreads, making soft sticky sounds as I increase my pace to keep up with Alessio's reflected hand.

Dante shoots me a glance in the mirror, catching my face ripe with voyeuristic lust. Puckering my lips, I blow him a kiss, returning his wordless "I love you" with my own. He's too far away for me to touch, yet I feel so connected to my Dante as our pleasures build to a cliff's edge I know we'll tumble from in mere moments.

My moans turn to a steady hum of pleasure as the tingles start to multiply at my center, my climax dangerously close to consuming me. Unable to tear my eyes from the mirror, I watch intently as Dante's body shakes and shudders, gasping for breath in Alessio's chokehold.

Transfixed, I watch as Dante comes on the mirror, his face contorting in pleasure as the cum streaks the reflective surface. What a dazzling sight: my good boy finally letting himself be free.

But I can't keep my focus on the mirror.

Dante's loud moans send me over the edge and I close my eyes, letting the waves of pleasure wash over me—crashing, crashing, crashing into me as goosebumps spread over my skin like fire. For a moment, maybe two, I just let myself enjoy the trembling sensation, feeling every feeling as I let it overwhelm me in the most glorious fashion.

When I finally open my eyes again, after who knows how long (or short), the naked men are embracing each other tightly, Dante's large frame spooned against Alessio's. My darling sub smiles at me in the mirror and I beam with pride.

My breathing is still rapid when Dante comes back to me and kneels on the carpet. I take his face in both hands, kissing him deeply as we share all the words we could never speak, not yet.

I feel so close to him in this moment, closer than ever.

"May I?" he asks, and I nod, brushing his hair from his face affectionately. He doesn't have to elaborate on what he wants; we want the same thing.

Dante lowers his mouth to my cunt, lapping at my sensitive clit as he swallows my orgasm. I moan softly, enjoying the sensation, but I stop him before he can work me into another delirium of lust.

"No more." I gasp, pulling Dante onto the bed beside me.

I catch Alessio's eye and he returns my smile, stroking his cock slowly, almost absentmindedly, as he watches us.

"You too. Come here," I invite him over and he joins us on the bed, Dante nestled between us.

With a contented sigh, I put my head on Dante's bare chest, listening for the steady rhythm of his heartbeat.

On the other side, Alessio places his head next to mine, cradled in Dante's right arm as I am in his left. Lazily, he entwines his fingers with mine, holding my hand over Dante's naked waist.

The last thing I remember before drifting asleep is Dante sweetly kissing the top of my head.

This was not how I had planned our Valentine's Day, but it was perfect, so, so perfect.

I'll ask him another time...

**Unsent Letter #6

I went back one more time. You never knew about it. Because you weren't there. I risked it all and took a normal flight—reckless, careless, desperate.

My mind was a mess with memories of you; feelings of you touching me, singing to me, making up nonsense riddles that neither of us knew answers to.

I wanted you to hold me as we danced close; to feel your need for me; for you to feel mine. I wanted to watch you smile; to kiss the laughter from your lips; to overdose on the intoxicating sound of your whispers.

Most of all, I wanted you to hold my hand, to tell me we'd be okay.

But you weren't there and I wasn't safe. Banned for life, they reminded me of when your asshole brother broke my jaw.

Just tell me where he is, I pleaded, I have to know.

He just laughed and told me that you'd been taken somewhere they would toughen you up, "fix" you, he said. But you weren't the one who needed fixing, the world did. Everything was broken without you.

Get out and never come back, he said. Leave or die, Dante. The Feras aren't welcome in Vegas, especially not you, you sick fuck.

Those didn't hurt as much as his final words.

He doesn't want to see you, he said. It was all a mistake, a foolish whim of youth. You meant nothing to him.

Nothing.

CHAPTER FIFTEEN

CONFESSIONS

DANTE...

A s the dark sky slowly turns grey outside, I don't know what to feel, but I feel it all at once—and it's amazing. And surreal. So fucking surreal. *What just happened?*

I hold Danica close as she sleeps with her head on my chest, stroking her back as I watch her tired body snore lightly. My beautiful, adventurous Queen. She calls me the "fearless" one she's clearly the fearless one.

Meanwhile, draped in my other arm, the-one-who-got-away, my first love, fucking Alessio Santoro himself, plays with my chest hair, his fingers weaving through the short curls. Finally having him in my arms still feels like a dream. If it is, I don't want to wake up.

"I've wanted this for so long, longer than you know," Alessio confesses, whispering against my chest to not wake Danica. But only because he doesn't know how deeply my *Tesoro* sleeps. It would take a lot of noise to wake Danica.

"How could you have? You're crazy," I reply with a smile, kissing his hair and catching a waft of green apples, an interesting choice for shampoo. But it's clearly working, because his long, wavy hair is so magnificent, so soft—I like touching it. It was never this long before, only down to his shoulders.

"I may be crazy, but you're still hard." Alessio grins, playfully reaching for my cock and shocking it from semi-erect to fully.

I shrug, moving his hand back to my chest before he works me up into another horny delirium. "Can you blame a man in this position?"

"You mean sandwiched between two irresistible beings?" Alessio suggests, giving me a wink. At least he never lost that playful side, even after all this time.

So much time...I want to focus on the here and now, but it's hard to stay in the present when the past is clawing at my insides.

"I looked for you, you know." I sigh. "Back then. I came back but you were gone."

Alessio stares into the distance, letting the silence hang between us for a moment. "My dad thought he could cure me of this *phase*, I had no choice." He no longer sounds playful.

"Your stupid brother broke my jaw."

"I know. What a twat. He hasn't changed at all. I'm sorry." Alessio kisses my neck, breathing into my ear so seductively that my cock stands as upright as the hairs on my skin as he adds: "But I'm not sorry you came back for me. I knew you cared."

"Some good that did. I really thought that we could run away and figure something out. How naive," I admit, looking away, my face flushed.

"I thought the same. It's what kept me sane during all those weeks at that fucked-up straight camp." It's Alessio's turn to sigh, his brows knitting in a frown.

All the rejection I realize I never got over pushes up in my throat, refusing to let me enjoy the moment. "You could've called me, sent me a letter...I don't know, reached out somehow?"

"I wanted to, more than anything. But when I came back, things were different. You were no longer *my* Dante; you were the great and mighty Don Fera, surrounded by an army."

"I didn't want to be—"

He doesn't let me finish. "I know, darling. Our fates were sealed long before. I couldn't risk them hurting you again."

My chest expands as I bask in Alessio's words. It was never rejection. Just the fucking mob interfering—as usual.

"I wish it was different." After all those years we lost, I can't believe we're getting our second chance.

"It couldn't have happened any other way. But we're here now. It's all that matters." Alessio the Wise.

Pulling him even closer, I kiss him tenderly, sweetly, savoring how his lips feel against mine. He's right, this is all that matters.

"I wrote you a letter once, I—" I start, ready to confess it all, but I never get to finish the thought.

Without warning, we're interrupted by a loud commotion downstairs.

Before any of us have time to move, the bedroom door explodes open, torn from its hinges, as four men in black ski masks storm in, guns drawn.

Alessio's body stiffens against mine, muscles taut with tension. Beside me, Danica jerks awake, her fingers clutching at me in panic. I pull her close, wrapping her in the sheets to shield her from these intruders' leering eyes. She fell asleep in just her panties, her clothes scattered carelessly around the room.

Without saying anything, the masked men hold their ground at the doorway, guns unwavering, a wall of menace. My mind races. *What the fuck is happening?* The air feels thick, pregnant, as if the room itself is holding its breath.

A dreadful silence falls, punctuated only by the muffled thud of approaching footsteps. My skin prickles with a cold dread as the goons part, making way for their leader.

The temperature seems to plummet, though I know it's not actually possible.

It's *him*.

For the second time tonight, I'm staring at a ghost. But this apparition doesn't stir longing; it churns my stomach with revulsion. The nightmare I dreaded when Danica opened those window blinds on the runway has materialized. Evil has found me. *Fuck.*

Francesco Santoro smiles like the cunt he is, his gun still firmly tucked in its holster. What time gave to the one brother, it stole from the other—he looks old, leathery almost. But it is unmistakably him. That voice still echoes in my ears after all these years.

"Dante Fera. What a surprise," Alessio's brother says, each word dripping with venom as he approaches the bed.

I'm acutely aware of my nakedness, of my vulnerability. Not only am I in his territory—a place from which he personally banished me—but I'm in bed with his younger brother, the very act that cost me a broken jaw years ago.

But I'm not 19 years old anymore...I don't have to be scared of this asshole.

Despite my resolve, I'm painfully conscious of my lack of a weapon. Danica's presence only heightens my anxiety. She shouldn't be dragged into this. Keeping her safe is my top priority, but it's not my only mission.

"Don Santoro, fancy meeting you here," I say slowly, my voice tight with controlled fury.

"You shouldn't leave your credit card details lying around veterinary clinics, Don Fera...just a tip," Francesco sneers, relishing in my discomfort.

"Oh god, I'm so sorry," Danica whispers, her voice trembling with guilt. But it's not her fault, it's mine.

I squeeze her hand reassuringly, then do something incredibly stupid, reckless really: I stand up, locking eyes with Francesco. His gaze flicks over me, a cruel smirk playing on his lips as he inspects my naked figure. Ignoring him, I reach for a pair of Alessio's pants hanging on a nearby armchair, pulling them on without bothering with underwear. My defiance is a small, stubborn victory.

"Some *weapon* you have there." Francesco scoffs. "Pity you use it for nefarious means."

"Do we have a problem?" I walk right up to him, my chest almost touching his. Despite being quite a bit taller than him, the advantage is worthless without a gun in hand.

"Say, Don Fera...Didn't I tell you never to come back?" Francesco jabs his finger into my chest, pushing me.

"Don't touch me, Francesco." I clench my fists, trying to keep the rising anger at bay. This asshole took so much from me. He had no right.

"Ha! You see those guys behind me, don't you? This isn't about what *you* want." His breath smells like onions and corruption. I hate him even more than before. Before I blamed myself for what happened, but now I know better, now I know it was never my fault.

It happens so quickly—all those years of pent-up anger surge through me like a tidal wave. I grab Francesco by the collar, yanking his face close to mine, my fury boiling over. In that instant, I'm ready to unleash a punch 25 years in the making.

I'd probably be dead within the minute if not for two things: Francesco halting his gunmen with a single gesture, and Alessio's unexpected grip on my shoulder.

"Dante! Don't!" Alessio's voice cuts through the red haze of my rage. He wedges himself between me and his brother. I hadn't even seen him get up from the bed, still completely naked.

"Aww, saved by your little *boyfriend*. Don't worry, I'll deal with you later." Francesco tries to shove his brother aside, but Alessio stands firm.

"No, Francesco. You made this choice for me all those years ago, but I'm not letting you make it again." Alessio's voice is steady, defiant. He shakes off Francesco's grip. "Leave Dante alone."

None of us see the gun until it's too late. Alessio must have hidden it nearby, ready for a moment like this. In a swift, calculated move, he presses the cold metal barrel against Francesco's ugly forehead.

"Don't you fucking move!" Alessio's threat reverberates through the room as he holds Francesco in front of him like a human shield. The gunmen, caught off guard, hesitate before lowering their weapons, their eyes darting between the brothers.

The room is a tense standoff, the air thick with unspoken threats and the weight of years of resentment. Francesco's confident facade cracks, a flicker of fear crossing his face. Alessio's resolve is unyielding, his grip on the gun steady.

For a moment, time stands still as the new power balance sinks in, and then Alessio turns to me with urgency. "Get out of here."

"I can't leave you, not again," I say with conviction. "Let me help you."

Francesco laughs out loud at this but doesn't say anything, muted by the metal against his brain.

"No, *amore mio*, go. Take Danica." Alessio squeezes my hand, but I stubbornly pull away.

"Alessio—"

"No. I won't let my brother near you again. Just get out of here. Use the secret tunnel behind the bookcase."

"How, I—"

"Just pull the copy of *Dante's Inferno*, and it will open. I'll hold them off. Just go."

I have so many questions. I want to ask about the choice of book. About what is going on. But Danica's panicked crying behind me refocuses my priorities. I have to get her out of here.

My insides are torn. I want to stay by Alessio's side, to fight with him. But I know I can't risk Danica's life, never again. This is not her battle.

"*Addio*, my loves." Alessio blows us a kiss before returning his focus to the assailants.

It's now or never. I meet Danica's gaze, and she nods; she's ready, bedsheet wrapped around her body like a toga.

We run towards the other room as fast as we can, not bothering with shoes or jackets.

The bookcase opens as instructed, leading down a long, narrow corridor that lights up as we pass through. *How many secret lovers have passed through these corridors?* I wonder without entertaining the thought for long; I don't want to know.

I hold tightly onto Danica's hand, our fingers interlaced, as we sprint down the corridor, our bare feet slapping against the cold, hard cement floor. The echo of gunshots reverberates through the walls behind us, growing fainter with each step.

My heart aches to turn back, to save Alessio, but I can't. I can only save one. One or the other.

We push forward, adrenaline propelling us until we reach a staircase at the end of the hallway. We descend swiftly, our breaths ragged, leading us one floor down to Alessio's office. It's empty, unguarded—everyone is upstairs, drawn by the chaos. But that won't last long.

Nobody stops us as we dash for the elevator, or when we descend back into the near-empty club—the show long since over but not the party. Half-dressed and barefoot, we draw curious glances, but this isn't the kind of place where people ask questions.

The bouncer tries to block our exit when we reach the final door, but I quickly take care of him, outmaneuvering his sturdy but slow bulk to push past the fresh line of people outside.

We spill into the early morning, the bright colors of Vegas blurring around us. I flag down the closest taxi, urgency in my voice as I shout for the driver to hurry. As the cab speeds away, I clutch Danica's hand even tighter, my mind racing with thoughts of Alessio and the chaos we left behind.

We leave tonight, even if we have to drive. We've overstayed our welcome.

Beside me, Danica is still crying, her non-smear lipstick finally smeared. I wrap my arm around her protectively, gently rocking her trembling body.

"It's okay, *Tesoro*. We're safe now. Shh," I murmur, my voice a soothing whisper despite the tremor in my hands. I stroke her messy hair, trying to convince myself of the words I'm saying as much as her.

"What about Alessio?" she asks, voicing the question that haunts my mind on repeat.

"He'll be okay, don't worry," I lie for both our benefit. Yet guilt gnaws at me, a relentless ache that makes my palms sweaty despite the cool dawn breaking into morning outside. I can't shake the feeling that I've abandoned Alessio again, left him to face the wrath of his fucked-up family.

I had no choice.

And just like before, I find myself fleeing Vegas while every fiber of my being pines for the Dark Prince that is Alessio Santoro.

****UNSENT LETTER #7**

There was no sympathy for my wounds—physical or emotional. Man up, my dad said. Family first. A man should be a man, do manly things, fuck women.

A man doesn't fall on his knees, and definitely not before the enemy.

One day, this all will be yours, my father said, the entire family empire, all the businesses. You need to rule over it with an iron fist, with precision and focus.

They did you a favor, boy. Get him out of your head.

But I couldn't. Days turned to months to years, and still, on sunny days with gloomy moods, I found myself wondering what had happened to you, where you were.

They said you'd never come back. Others said you'd found The One, that you were happily raising your family abroad. Nobody said you'd missed me as much as I missed you, that I was something to you instead of just an impossible teenage conquest.

He took me to the whorehouse, my father. Tried to get them to fuck you out of my system as he forced me to give a stranger what I wanted you to take—my well-guarded innocence, my virginity.

I felt nothing, nothing but disgust, emptiness...used. No matter how I fought it, I was trapped in a destiny I didn't want but couldn't escape. My future wasn't my own. If it was, it would be full of you.

But time passed and you never came back.

What did it matter what I wanted?

Life was all about managing your disappointments, Dante, my father said.

Chapter Sixteen

Aftershock

Danica...

My breath doesn't return to its normal rhythm until we close our bedroom door behind us. Home at last, with our hastily packed suitcases strewn across the room.

The angst still clings to my throat as I collapse onto our familiar four-poster bed, opening my arms for Dante to join me. He rests his head on my chest, his body trembling with unspoken emotions.

For a long time, I just hold him as he finally breaks down, his sobs muffled against my breasts. I stroke his disheveled hair that still smells like pussy and regret.

How Emilio managed it, what strings he pulled, remains a mystery. But we were packed and out of Vegas in under an hour, permission for take-off granted without question. The pilot didn't say anything this time. No one did.

We'd changed our clothes on the plane, a futile attempt to feel fresh. As the sun rose higher outside the small oval windows, neither of us could sleep or speak. We just stared into the distance, exhausted, holding each other's hands tightly, trying to make sense of the whirlwind of a night we just experienced.

I want to tell Dante it will be okay, but I can't promise that. He dared to hope, only to have his heart shattered again, still a prisoner to his inescapable fate. And me? I'm lost in my own thoughts, the memory of Alessio's lips on mine still fresh, his jovial laughter echoing in my mind. Even though we've only just met, I crave his presence like an addiction.

I kiss Dante's hair, my lips lingering there. Time becomes meaningless as the sun climbs higher in the sky, but the curtains are drawn tight, enveloping us in a comforting darkness. The dim light of the bedside lamp casts soft shadows around the room, sheltering us in a fragile sense of peace amidst the chaos we've left behind.

"I don't know what to do," Dante finally breaks the silence, his voice small like a little boy as he clings to me. My heart breaks for the umpteenth time today; I can't bear to see him like this.

"I'm so sorry, baby. We should never have gone to Vegas," I say softly, trying to keep the tears from my voice. I feel so guilty, so tired, so confused—all the things at once.

I want a different ending, not this one. Dante deserves better. We all do.

Once more I find myself worrying about Alessio's fate, whether he is even still alive. It is a difficult thought.

"It's not your fault. How could you have known? I never told you. I never told anyone," Dante says. He holds onto me tightly as he speaks, eyes closed.

Holding myself back, I don't say anything, just give him space to find the words.

When Dante finally manages to start speaking, there is no containing the spillage. It gushes into the space between us like a flood as I stroke his hair.

"I didn't even think about sex much, you know, when I was younger. For a while, I thought I was asexual," he starts, and I try to imagine my tattooed god as a young boy.

Try as I might, I struggle to picture this sex-crazed man of mine as a confused teenager.

Dante slowly continues his story, stopping from time to time to find the right translation in his mind. *I really should get on this learning Italian thing,* I think to myself as he lays his broken pieces out in the open, shard by shard.

"I retreated from the world after my mom died. But Alessio changed that. He stirred something in me that I didn't know could be stirred. I don't know when it changed; when I stopped seeing him as a friend and started seeing him as the one I wanted to take my honor."

So many questions fill my mind, but I don't interrupt him. I knew Dante lost his virginity to some chick he never even knew the name of, but I always thought that it was by choice. I would never have predicted that Dante was hiding a forbidden love story.

He tells me how they used to go to Vegas often back then. Apparently, the Santoros used to be close allies of the Feras. How quickly things change.

"Alessio and I always found the grown-up talk boring, concocting some excuse or another to sneak away. When we were younger, it was to the movies or extravagant music performances. We liked the same songs..." Dante's voice is monotonous as he unravels his painful memories, pausing from time to time to take a deep breath. But he doesn't stop, no matter how drained we are.

"That final time, before the turf war turned our families against each other, that time was different. Alessio was 18 then; I was already 19—we were no longer goofy kids who liked to share made-up ghost stories whispered into each other's ears. No, I wanted him to whisper other things in my ear, dirty things, things I couldn't say out loud."

I scratch Dante's back, lazily trailing my nails over his shirt in an attempt to soothe him.

"It was okay to want those things," I tell him, finally saying something.

"My dad didn't think so. He was determined that I behave how he imagined a future-Don should behave. He was such a hard man—bitter, mean. I don't know why my mom stayed with him. She was a true angel who loved me no matter what."

"She sounds lovely. You never told me what happened to her?" I ask. But today's not the day for that story. One skeleton at a time.

Dante continues like he didn't hear me, but we both know he did. "My favorite thing was spending time with her in the kitchen. It was way more exciting than going on business outings with my dad. She taught me how to knit even..." Dante's voice trails off.

"You can knit? That's amazing. You never told me," I fill the space, encouraging him.

"Probably not anymore. My dad quickly put a stop to it when he found me sitting by my mother's feet with a pair of knitting needles, watching soap operas and laughing about silly things. My mom had a great sense of humor."

"She sounds like a lovely person."

"My mom was the best. She would have loved you. We could've gone on those elaborate island holidays you love so much, like a family...if she was still here."

"I wish I could have met her," I reply, even though it sounds stupid out loud.

"She was so beautiful. Luca got her eyes—it's hard to look at him sometimes. I got her smile. But I lose it some times," Dante continues in his faraway voice, lost in his mind as he bares his soul.

"I love your smile." I stroke his cheek, touching the corners of his mouth that are far from smiling now.

"My dad didn't. Children should be seen and not heard, he'd say whenever he heard us laugh. He said a lot of things. They were always fighting, my parents. They had very different parenting styles. My mom wanted me to have a childhood, my dad wanted me to toughen up. I used to love playing guitar, but he smashed that to pieces within weeks."

"What a dick, I'm so sorry, baby." And I thought *my* father was shit. Dante's father sounds worse.

"Oh, that's nothing." Dante laughs sadistically, a pained look settling on his brow. "When I was 11, he found me baking cupcakes in the kitchen. It was the year after my mom died. I was so scared when he came in, I ran away from him, ran to the stables, to my best friend. Allegro…"

"Your safe word." It finally makes sense. I've asked him why he chose Allegro as his safe word so many times before, but his answers remained vague.

"Yeah. Such a stunning thoroughbred horse. My mom got him for me on my sixth birthday, when Luca was still a toddler. I thought my dad wouldn't find me there, that I'd be safe with Allegro. How naive of me…" Dante trails off, his voice choking up.

"What happened to Allegro?" I ask, scared of the answer.

"My dad found me eventually. By that time, he was furious. He didn't even hesitate. He just pulled out his gun and shot the horse. I screamed and shouted at him, but he didn't give a fuck. He just shot Allegro and walked away, telling me how it was my own fault."

I gasp audibly, I can't help it. "No, Dante. No. Surely not?"

"My dad didn't care about children or animals. He didn't care about anything but the business. He shot Allegro and told me to grow up. He said that Feras don't cry, that I'd better do what he said, or else…And then he walked away, no remorse, nothing. He just left me there, a sobbing 11-year-old, holding my dead horse for hours and hours until Emilio finally carried me home like a baby."

My heart shatters into a million pieces for Dante. I cannot even begin to imagine what that must have done to a poor child, to anyone.

"I'm so sorry, *Tesoro*..." I can't hold back my tears any longer. They come streaming down my face, wetting Dante's hair as I hold him against my chest, confiding his secrets into my bosom that probably still holds traces of Alessio's cum.

For a while, we just hold each other, letting the tears stain our cheeks without resistance. The moment is so heavy, almost crushing, but I force myself to be present, to sit with it.

It's Dante who finds the words first, the Pandora's Box of his past finally unlocked.

"I probably deserved it. I'm a bad man, Danica; I've done so many bad things. I didn't want to tell you because deep down I knew you wouldn't want me anymore if you discovered all the secrets I'd buried. I'm not worthy of a Goddess like you..."

I've had Dante tied up in the most humiliating positions imaginable, exposed, at my mercy to use as I please, but never in any of those situations have I seen the great Don Fera this vulnerable, like a lost child.

I feel useless; there is nothing I can do to protect him from a past that's already happened, long before I was even born.

"Oh, baby. I still want you. I want all of you, even the broken parts. I love you, Dante Fera, even your darkness, your pain, your sadness." Gently, I lift his head to face me, wet eyes meeting wet eyes.

Dante sighs. "Oh, Danica. I love you too, so much. I suck at words, but it's so much. I will be better, I promise, I'll tell you things..."

I kiss him sweetly, moving my lips to his cheeks and brushing the tears away.

"Whenever you're ready, *Tesoro*. I will always be here to listen. Here to distract you or soothe you or beat the shit out of you until the pain blacks out everything—whatever you need, I'm here."

"Thank you. Just thank you." Dante looks at me gratefully, his eyes are red and swollen. I don't know when last he just let himself cry, cry without trying to cover the pain with anger—the only acceptable emotion for a man, they say. *Fuck that.*

There is nothing left to say but a lot to process.

"I think we should watch some *Parks & Rec* until we fall asleep. It's been a long night," I suggest, stroking Dante's hair.

"Can't it be something else? You know that show and I are not friends," Dante protests, slowly coming back to the present.

"Nope. Shh now, baby." I grin, pulling him back to my chest. "If you stop whining, I might even let you suck on a titty while we watch."

"Ah, well, you know *Parks* is my favorite show." He smiles faintly, his face etched with the weariness of exhaustion.

"Such a little shit sometimes." I shake my head as I reach for the remote.

Before the opening credits finish rolling over the screen, Dante is asleep against my chest.

I let the episode run through, and then another.

I'm beyond exhausted, but I can't stop thinking about that little boy and his dead horse...

**UNSENT LETTER #8

It's all on you now, Emilio said, putting his hand on my shoulder as we watched them pull the blanket over my father's dead body.

I can't, Emilio, I'm not ready, I protested, panic pushing up in my throat.

They closed his eyes and took him away, leaving an empty bed and a lot of responsibility.

It was mere months since you fucked my mouth in that dingy club in Vegas, mere months since I lost all hope in a moment, as soon as your brother walked through the door.

But I know now that I didn't lose it all that day, that I had more to lose.

I'm sorry, kid, but you have no choice, Emilio said, squeezing my shoulder as tears rolled down my eyes, tears I would never be allowed to show anyone again, but Emilio knew.

It's your job to keep them all alive now, he bestowed the future I knew I couldn't escape upon me like a heavy mantle.

It pushed everything else down, took up all the space, crushed any dreams I had of finding a space for us to escape to and be free. It was a matter of life and death and my freedom could mean their death.

We were never meant to be. All those years we spent growing up together, turning into men, men with needs and desires, men with feelings for each other. We came from the same world, you understood me. But what brought us together would forever keep us apart.

I wept for more than just my father that day. I wept for the loss—the loss of myself, of what I could have been, what I could have been with you by my side.

Goodbye, my Dark Prince.

Goodbye, Alessio.

CHAPTER SEVENTEEN

RESTLESS

DANTE...

The pavement thuds under my feet in the crisp morning air, each impact jarring through muscles still heavy from sleeping nearly 22 hours straight. We'd barely managed to stay conscious long enough to eat at 2 AM before collapsing back into bed.

But even after all that rest, my mind feels raw, exposed.

My phone's weight against my arm feels strange—I never run with it, but the desperate need for news about Alessio overrides routine. Every hour without word makes the knot in my stomach tighter. Emilio's been working connections non-stop, but so far, nothing but shadows.

It's an unknown number but I pick it up anyway, stopping dead in my tracks as the voice I long for most greets me casually. *"Amore mio..."*

His voice hits me like a punch in a the gut. "Alessio!" Relief floods my system so fast it makes me dizzy. "Are you okay?" I quickly add.

"I'm fine. Well, mostly." Exhaustion threads through his familiar drawl.

"Are you hurt?"

"Just a shot to the thigh. I've had worse." His laugh carries no humor.

"Jesus. What happened?"

"Let's just say it's a long story that involves a lot of brotherly betrayal." A heavy pause. "I knew Francesco was plotting something, but I thought we'd have more time. I'm sorry you and Danica got caught in our family's mess."

"I thought I'd lost you. Again." The confession tears free before I can stop it.

"Ah! You *do* care. I knew it." His attempt at levity falls flat against my raw nerves.

"You could have been killed."

"Could've, but it turns out my brother's not as popular as he thinks. Two of the guards were already mine."

"A coup?"

"Something like that." His voice hardens. "It was planned, but Francesco finding out you were in town forced our hand. We weren't ready. But once you and Danica were clear..." Pride creeps into his tone. "My people made their move. Some bullets flew, but we had backup waiting."

Relief makes my knees weak. Alessio alive. Alessio safe. Everything else is details.

"Where's Francesco?"

"Somewhere he won't be troubling anyone again." Steel beneath silk. "Far from Vegas and *my* empire."

"*Your* empire?"

"Good morning, Don Fera!" His voice shifts into an absurd British accent. "Don Santoro speaking. How may I be of service?" His laughter bubbles through the line as the implications hit me. Francesco's reign is over.

"Congratulations? Alessio—"

"Come back to Vegas, darling." All pretense drops from his voice.

"The Feras are banned from Vegas, remember?"

"Not anymore. You'll be treated like royalty, I promise." His voice softens. "Besides, I need more Danica in my life. That one's a keeper. I'd gladly kneel before a woman like that."

"Danica is amazing," I agree.

For a minute, the line is quiet. This is the part where I tell him when I'll see him, or at the very least give him the reason I can't come. But I don't say anything. It all feels like a lot.

Alessio sighs softly, barely audible, but I hear. "You'll always have a home this side. Whenever you're ready. I probably have some healing to do myself."

"Alessio..." I start, but I can't find the words, not in any language.

"Sì?"

I chicken out. "Nothing. I'll tell you in person one day."

"I don't regret any of it—just know that." Alessio's voice softens with a rare tenderness.

"Me neither."

"See you soon, *amore mio*. Send Queen Danica my regards."

"I will. She's very worried about you."

"I know. I'll make it up to her, to both of you. Soon."

"Soon."

There is so much more I want to say, want to hear, but we let the silence hang between us for a few more seconds before I end the call.

I force myself to start running again as the thoughts overwhelm my mind, cluttering the space until they finally start falling into order the further away I get, the more I sweat in the mid-morning sun.

Part of me wants to rush off to Vegas immediately, to throw myself into Alessio's arms. But the more distance

I get from the moment, the more I realize the Alessio I wanted then is not the Alessio offering himself to me now. More importantly, I'm not the same Dante anymore. I have lived so much since 19; I've seen so much death, so much pain...

I'm in love with the idea of Alessio more than the reality of him, I see that now. When you've had 25 years to obsess over anything, there is no longer any way for the reality to live up to that fantasy, to that idea of a person you held close all those years ago.

Sure, I still want to fuck Alessio senseless, to lose myself in his passion, the chaotic rollercoaster that is his world...but I can't see myself coming home to Alessio, baring my soul and crying in his arms. No, I don't want that from him.

There is only one person who I trusted with all parts of me—Danica.

There is no denying that I am the best version of me around her, the me I want to be, the me she believes I could still be...like my mom believed.

Danica knows me so well, better than anyone ever has—even my dead wife who spent seven years trying to unravel the darkness inside me. Yet Danica does it so effortlessly, without even trying. She just loves so freely, so unapologetically. I don't have to think about who to be around her, or how to hide myself like I've done all my life.

She may be young and sometimes a complete brat, but the effect she has on my body, my mind, my soul, is unmatched. Even when I'm grumpy or try to push her away, to bury myself in work, Danica will drag me from my desk, forcing me into stupid pajamas to watch some or other show I don't care about. But I like it when she holds me, when she strokes my hair, when she lets me suckle on her breasts.

Sitting down to watch TV was not something I usually did, but with Danica, I'd watch (almost) anything. Especially when she milks me dry during *Doctor Who* reruns, stroking my cock until I have no liquids left to spill for her, dry and sensitive, overstimulated, but my mind clear.

I used to think she didn't actually enjoy seeing me get off; that she's just pretending, but Danica was sincere, a real pleasure Domme. She once made me do some dumb love language quiz with her and it said her love language was gifts, mine was physical touch—whatever that means.

Maybe that's why, with just one touch, she is the one who can calm the chaos and tame the darkness—even if just for a while. Danica doesn't run away from me, from who I am. She doesn't tell me to be different; no, she opens her arms to me and welcomes me into her bosom, no matter what state I'm in or how bloody my hands are. She doesn't make me feel ashamed. All she wants is to be with me.

I stop running, my thoughts finally in order. The answer is as clear as day—I want to spend my days making Danica happy, treating her like the Goddess she is. My Queen of pain and pleasure. I want to share everything with her, the good and the bad, the messy, the painful.

Danica is more than a Queen; she is my person. I know that now. I want to make her mine forever and always, my wife—Missus Danica Fera.

The thought makes me smile. It sounds right.

Still, it doesn't make me want Alessio less...

Three months later...

Chapter Eighteen

DO-OVER

Danica...

I can't believe we're back in Vegas. On stage, an effeminate man with a dog mask and caged cock grovels on the floor, ass in the air, kissing the shiny leather shoes of the Dominatrix.

My head jerks back every few minutes to make sure nobody is about to press a gun into my back. But this time, we are here openly—without masks, without threat. Quite the opposite actually, we are super protected thanks to Alessio, or "Don Santoro" as he goes by now.

Our jovial Joker isn't here, though. We have Vegas all to ourselves this time. Something about an ongoing internal fight between those who wanted him in charge and those stubborn ones still trying to get his brother back on the throne. He is hiding out at some undisclosed safe house for now while his men deal with the threat.

I'm disappointed we won't get to see him, but I'm also glad to finally have my Vegas do-over with Dante.

The past three months have been hard, but such a bonding experience at the same time. I feel closer to Dante than ever. Our shared desire for Alessio has unlocked a whole new level in our relationship.

Dante has also been doing a lot of work on learning how to express a wider spectrum of emotions, an ongoing struggle. Well, he was doing that, *and s*pending a lot of time on his knees.

My own time has been filled with combat sports and strength training at ungodly hours, finally fitting in some proper shooting practice too. If I'm going to spend my life with a man like Dante Fera, I need to know how to protect myself—that much is clear.

But there is no training today, at least not any of the sporty kind. Today is a special day.

Looking away from the scene in the lit-up room before us, from the sub-boy squirming on the floor, so desperate, I squeeze Dante's hand.

He smiles, turning his full attention to me. "Let's go back to our room, *Tesoro*," Dante suggests. "I've seen enough. I don't want this; I just want you."

"So, translation: you're horny as fuck and you want me to do something about it?" I grin, patting the obvious tent in his pants.

He blushes, I can tell by his body language even if I can't see the color of his cheeks in the dark room.

I check my watch. It's still early. But I'll stall some other way.

"Such a silly old man. Come on then." I feign a dramatic sigh, getting up with my body hunched over to not block anyone's view of the stage.

"Who are you calling old?" Dante scoffs, grabbing me without much effort and chucking me over his shoulder. I squeal, rousing some disapproving looks from other audience members, but I pay them no mind, pounding my fists on Dante's back as he carries me out the door like a caveman, much to my delight.

"I'm going to make you pay for this!" I threaten playfully as Dante throws me into the nearest taxi and orders the driver to our hotel. It is a different one from where we stayed before, even nicer.

This time Dante booked everything. It was *his* idea that we return. I was hesitant but quickly swayed by the allure of the neon capital.

I was relieved that Alessio was okay but surprised that Dante didn't want to go back immediately after he got that phone call. It was hard to completely push down the fear of him leaving me for Alessio eventually. But Dante assured me that I was the only one for him.

Sure, he was open to play partners and wanted to spend more time with Alessio, but I was the one he wanted to come home to—that's what he said when he got back all sweaty from his run that morning, ambushing me while I was still fast asleep. It was a heartwarming sentiment, especially from someone like him, someone who usually chose their words carefully.

As the taxi pulls up to our hotel, way faster than I thought it would, I check my watch again. We're an hour too early but I'm silently praying to no deity in particular that everything has already been set up, that it's ready.

Waving my hands about, I stop Dante as he's about to push open the door to our suite nestled high in the vibrant sky. "Wait, let me!"

He smiles but steps aside, nonetheless. "You're being weird."

"Just wait outside," I demand, rushing in and closing the door behind me quickly. Trust Dante to mess up my carefully laid plans, again.

But as I survey the room, it's clear that everything is ready, just as I ordered. The question is, am I ready?

Show time! I take a deep breath and try to calm the heart palpitations that appear out of nowhere before calling Dante inside.

The door swings open and Dante freezes in the doorway, taking in his unexpected surroundings.

"Danica, what the—" Dante stares at the transformed room in amazement, unable to finish his sentence.

I blush, closing the door behind him. "I wanted a bit more of an *intimate* setting."

The room is filled with candles floating in glass bowls, creating a romantic atmosphere of shadow and flame. Every free surface is covered with candles—even the floor: a candlelit path leads from the door to the bed scattered with red rose petals. From the ceiling, woven strings of fairy lights drip down above our heads.

"It's so special." Dante smiles, taking me into his arms and hugging me tight.

"Those are for you," I say, pointing to glass bottles hanging amidst the fairy lights, dangling just above Dante's tall figure but far out of reach for me. It looks exactly how I'd imagined it when I'd shared my carefully detailed plan with the staff in secrecy earlier while Dante was napping.

"What are they?" Dante asks, touching the bottle closest to him.

"Take them down and read them, in that order." With a nervous smile, I watch intently as Dante rips the first bottle off its string. Inside, a rolled-up note, handwritten, waits to be fished out.

My mouth is dry, my hands the opposite. I want to look away but eagerly await Dante's reaction to my elaborate gesture. Time slows to a near-halt as he reads the note.

Dante looks at the note and back to me. "Danica," is all he says, placing the note against his heart.

"Read it out loud." I cross my arms and uncross them again, not sure what to do with all this nervous tension. I've thought about this moment so many times.

"*You are the reason for my breathing and the light in the darkness, Dante Fera,*" he reads slowly, the paper close to his face in the candle-lit space.

He wants to say something but I need him to unbottle the rest first. I can't wait any longer.

"And the next one!"

Dante grabs another bottle, reading its message out loud. "*My darling boy, I want to spend forever making you happy.*"

One by one Dante reads my soppy declarations of love, my confessions of desire—12 of them in total. When he loosens the final bottle from its string, I know my time has come. I take a deep breath and get in position.

When Dante turns around, note in hand, I'm on my knees, the little black velvet box stretched out to him. I don't need him to read me this note, I repeat the words myself: "Will you make me the happiest woman in the world and marry me, Don Fera?"

Dante laughs and drops to his knees unexpectedly, hugging me close.

"Is that a yes?" I ask, eager to know. This is not really how I expected him to react. *What's he doing on the floor?*

But then Dante pulls a little box from his jacket pocket, one not too dissimilar to the one I'm holding out to him. "Only if you marry me, Miss Matthews."

Finally realizing what was going on, I burst out laughing too, my nervousness all gone. "You were going to propose as well?"

"Why do you think we're back in Vegas." Dante shrugs sheepishly, popping open the box to reveal the most elegant golden band I've ever seen, decorated with a ginormous diamond. It is perfect, so perfect.

"That's so romantic, baby." Happy tears burn my eyes, threatening to spill down my cheeks.

Dante runs his hand through his hair, looking about as anxious as I am. "So, shall we?"

"Yes, yes, and another yes!" I wrap my arms around him jubilantly, sloppily kissing his face all over.

Still on our knees on the fancy carpet, the candles flickering beside us, we slide each other's rings on at the same time.

This is not how I'd imagined the moment when I planned our first Valentine's Vegas trip—it was even better.

Finally!

Chapter Nineteen

TEACHER

Dante...

My cock is so hard, I feel like bursting.

But it isn't time yet.

"What a bad boy. You know Mistress doesn't like it when you don't do your homework," Danica says in her strict Teacher's voice, smacking a long wooden ruler in her hand dramatically. She towers over me in her heels, dressed in a short black pencil skirt with an oversized white shirt tied at her waist, unbuttoned, her large breasts only half covered.

Beneath her, I sit on a little wooden stool that is way too small for my broad figure. I'm bare except for knee-high fishnet stockings and my collar. I wear its chokehold not for her, but for me. I like how it feels around my neck. It makes me feel safe to be adorned in a physical reminder that I belong to someone. When I wear my collar, I can feel Danica's hands around my throat, holding me, always.

"I'm sorry, Miss. I've misbehaved," I say ashamedly, lowering my eyes to my erection that sticks out awkwardly between my spread thighs as I try to keep my balance on the tiny chair. I feel so exposed, so vulnerable before her. My stomach knots.

This is one of my favorite role-play scenes with Danica—the strict Teacher and the naughty student who needs to be taught a lesson. Luckily for me, she likes it too.

Temporary red lashes cover my thighs from the whip now discarded on the floor while an assortment of other implements lie waiting among the candle-lit surfaces of the space in which we proposed to each other not long ago.

"Disobedient boys don't get rewards," Danica says, pinning my cock between her heel and my stomach, grinding down on its head until I howl in pain.

She kicks me in the balls and I topple onto the floor, curling up in a fetal position. The aching pain in my dick is the only thing left in my mind, a blinding pulse that empties the chaos, my father's voice, everything.

"I'm...I'm sorry," I plead, holding my hands protectively in front of my junk. I know I can stop her at any time, I know my safe words—verbal and non-verbal.

But I don't want her to stop and we both know it. Nobody understands my body like Danica; it belongs to her.

"Words are not going to cut it, little puppy. Get up!" she orders, her voice assertive to the point of aggression. I don't dare question her, not when I'm in this state, not when she talks to me like this.

Danica grabs me by my collar and forces me to my feet, naked and awkward before her fully clothed figure.

"I'm sorry, I'm sorry. I'll do my homework next time," I plead as Danica grabs my cock and pulls me towards her, long nails purposefully digging into my hard, sensitive skin.

"Oh, we will make sure of it," my tormentor-slash-savior says.

Danica leads me to the bed by the cock, pulling too hard. Like the bad student I am, I follow her meekly, shuffling awkwardly over the plush black carpet.

As Danica sits down on the bed, she moves her hand lower, cupping my balls. My entire body shudders in fearful excitement.

"Please..." I whimper, knowing just how dangerous she can be.

Danica tugs, hard, and the wind leaves my lungs in a painful gasp. I topple over her, bending over her knees—just how she wants me.

She repositions herself to trap my cock between her thighs, holding it between clenched knees as I awkwardly reposition myself over her lap, feet on the floor on one side, hands on the other.

I am way too big for her to pull me over her lap, but this is not the kind of fact Danica gives a fuck about. She makes her own rules, the only requirement being that they match the ones negotiated in our contract.

"Some lessons you have to learn the hard way, it seems," Teacher-Danica says, caressing my ass in a move that makes my dick jump.

But I'm fooled. I know what's coming, and I brace myself, muttering more apologies as Danica brings her flat hand down with force.

"One," I count.

She's gotten better at spankings. My ass is on fire by the time she reaches smack number seven. By 13, it becomes uncomfortable.

Still, my erection does not let up. I'm so aroused, even more than I was before she pulled me over her lap. *How is that even possible?*

When the final smack (number 20) lands on my bare skin, I know my ass is bright red, her hand imprinted on my flesh.

I'm crying. Not from the pain, but because I feel small.

"Shh now, it's all over. I know you'll be a good student from now on, right?" Danica helps me up onto the bed beside her, cooing in a nurturing voice that is patronizingly sweet.

"I'll be good." I stop myself just in time from calling her *Mommy*. That's a different scene.

"It seems I have no choice. I'll have to fuck some sense into you." Danica shakes her head in mock disapproval, still in character.

"Please, Miss, no," I pretend not to want it even though I really do.

Danica never does anything without full consent, even when roleplaying non-consent scenes. Every detail is planned before, discussed at length. She knows I like to be treated rough sometimes.

"Shh, quiet. I want you to lie down and close your eyes." She grabs my balls threateningly, just to remind me what will happen if I don't listen.

I nod quickly, closing my eyes.

The anticipation kills me as I lie there waiting for her, all exposed. She could smack me at any time, or spit on me, or step on me. But it's none of those things—it's far more painful!

It takes me a second to register what is going on.

The pain is blinding, overwhelming, sharp...

"Keep 'em closed!" Danica warns as I squirm on the bed, howling in agony. I know I can shout *Allegro* at her, but I don't want to. I want her to hurt me. The pain feels almost soothing compared to the storm that never stops raging in my head.

I don't speak, don't say anything, just focus on a singular, beautiful thought—the pain!

Another drop of hot wax drips onto my cock, and I scream. I can think of nothing but the black dot of pain with the red edges that spread through my circuits, dulling everything in its path.

"Down, boy. This is not about your pleasure," Danica says, but we both know it is. It is ALL about my pleasure.

I keep my eyes closed as she pushes my stockinged legs down on my chest, as the cold lube touches my hole, as she slips a finger inside my ass, two, spreading me.

I keep my eyes closed but my mouth cannot stay quiet. I moan and whine and hum for her as Danica's fingers find their way to my prostate, curling over to hit that spot.

She pulls them out again suddenly and I gasp, empty.

"Look at me, boy," Danica demands, and I finally open my eyes to find her naked before me, pegging harness firmly secured to her body. The dildo she's chosen is large but not too large. We've played with bigger. She rubs it against my cock, hardness to hardness.

"I'm going to fuck you into oblivion, puppy. You won't be able to walk normally again for a week, and there is nothing you can do about that," Danica says, pressing her silicone cock to my entrance.

I don't move; I don't do anything other than hold my breath, waiting for her to push her lubed phallus inside me and make good on her promise of oblivion.

Danica grabs me by the collar, choking me, holding me in place as she slides her thick cock inside, slowly, until all of her is buried in my ass.

I am full, uncomfortable at first, sore, stretching to take it all. But then the pain slowly gives way to pleasure.

Desperate, I struggle for breath as Danica pulls out only to plunge back in, harder, deeper—again and again.

"You are mine. Always and forever," Danica says. She wraps her free hand around my wax-coated cock and starts to stroke in tandem with her hip thrusts, flooding my senses with pain and pleasure in a delirium that quickly builds to an orgasm I struggle to contain.

"I don't care who we play with or who we fuck, you'll always be mine," she tells me between gritted teeth as she squeezes my delicate balls.

"Please, Miss..." I can't finish my sentence but we both know what I want.

"No coming until I say so," the future-Missus-Fera insists, and I know my torture is far from over.

How did I get so lucky?

CHAPTER TWENTY

MINE

DANICA...

Bringing them to my lips, I kiss Dante's fingers one by one. I count each one, kissing and counting, until I've counted all 10. I count his ring finger again, marveling at how good it looks with a ring on it.

Mine.

I slip the entire finger into my mouth, ring and all, sucking the cold metal. It used to be the only ringless finger on that hand, but no more. Four rings of death, one ring of love—balance in the Fera household.

Around us, the sheets are a sticky mess of cum, lube, and sweat. But I don't care; I'm content. I rest my head on Dante's chest, my naked, spent body fully on top of his. Around us, the candles still flicker, surrounded by pools of wax.

It was a rough session, but those always have the most intimate aftercare scenes—for us at least. These were non-negotiable, the only way to bring Dante down slowly, back to me, to this realm. But they weren't just for Dante. My mind needed these moments to restore the equilibrium as well, to reconnect.

Of all the role-playing scenarios we've tried, Teacher-student is one of my favorites too. It's not possible to like it as much as Dante does, but it sure does get me wet as fuck. There's something about dolling out punishment that is really appealing to me.

But it's more than just punishing Dante. I'm not sadistic at all. Well, not toward Dante at least. He's the most important thing in my life. I don't get pleasure from hurting him. But I do get pleasure from that blissful look that falls over his face when he floats off to subspace.

That's what makes me feel powerful—being able to get him to that state; him trusting me enough to let go to that point. For a man like Dante Fera, trust is hard to come by. Who could blame him, considering the life he's led?

I initially thought I'd get bored with our kinky play, but the more we played, the more I thought about a long-term dynamic. Whatever weird fantasies I had; whatever games I thought up for us, Dante was always willing to humor me. Well, most times. Sounding was a step too far (now I know).

When it comes to his body, I know exactly what he needs. I know what buttons to push, how to drain the stress from his shoulders with the calculated lash of a whip. What I don't know, is how to give his mind what it needs. He always tells me how good our sessions are for his head, but I know some bruises cannot be fixed by new ones.

"You okay, baby?" I ask for the fourth time, seeking Dante's eyes.

My darling boy smiles, crisscrossing his fingers through mine to hold up our hands and marvel at our rings once more. His is a plain black titanium band—subtle, durable, sleek—while the diamond on mine is probably too expensive to wear outside without guards.

"I'm good, so good. Thank you, *Tesoro*. For everything." I know he means it. His expression is calm, at peace. It is a good look on him.

"And you, thank you," I say, lazily dragging my nails over his chest. "I feel stronger each time we play."

"This is who you were always meant to be—*La Donna Fera*."

"I like the sound of that. We can be our own family." I kiss his collarbone, trailing little silly kisses up and down his neck.

Is there any gift more beautiful, more complete, rarer, than Dante's submission? Nothing in the world.

Dante grins. "Speaking of family, I have a present for you. I hope you don't mind—"

"You better not be pregnant, Dante!" I tease and we both laugh.

"Not that kinda family." He reaches over to his phone and opens his chat with Emilio. "See, it's all been arranged."

Perplexed, I stare at the picture, swiping to the other multiples as I try to make sense of it. This is not what I expected.

"They didn't have anywhere to go with him. I thought you might like a friend." Dante smiles as I zoom in on the picture of the familiar dog, sitting in what is clearly our backyard, surrounded by lots of chew toys.

"Is that—?"

"Yup, the one from Vegas. I hope you don't mind. I had them fly him over and Emilio's been settling him in."

I laugh as the final photo pops up: an awkward selfie attempted by Emilio with the dog eagerly licking his face. The result is a blurred moment of absolute heartwarming gold.

My heart is so full, I feel like bursting. I've always wanted another dog but I didn't know if I could bear it, not after how mine died. But that was a long time ago; I'm ready now.

"I don't know what to say. It's so fucking cute!" I swipe over the pictures again, already trying out names in my head. Our first pet.

"Does that mean we can keep him?" Dante asks, still unsure how to read the situation. I guess getting pets isn't something he had planned either. Big, scary Don Fera with a little rescue mutt and Gen Z fiancé...it's a look, for sure.

The thought warms me from the inside. Chosen family hey. That's what everyone needs. You can't do shit about the family you're born into, but sometimes, if you're lucky, you find your crew...usually in the most unexpected places.

There is no question in my mind, we're definitely keeping the dog. I can't wait to go home and cuddle the shit out of it. Dante probably won't let it sleep inside, but I'll get him to come around.

"Yes! We're keeping him" I exclaim excitedly as I detangle myself from Dante.

Grabbing the headboard to help with my balance, I jump on the bed, watching with great joy as Dante just shakes his head like the old man I sometimes accuse him of being.

"You're going to get hurt, get down!" Dante calls, but I just laugh, sticking my tongue out at him as I jump even higher on the messy bed. Whoever said Dommes couldn't be brats needs to get over their obsession with labels and boxes.

Kicking my legs out under me, I let myself drop back onto the bed like I'm weightless, almost bouncing off the soft mattress. But luckily Dante catches me in the strong arms I'm going to wake up next to for the rest of our lives.

He's about to scold me about jumping on the bed, I know he is, but he doesn't get the chance. I smother his lips in mine, kissing him deeply. There is nowhere I would rather be.

A family of my own.

EPILOGUE

Nine Months Later...

CHAPTER TWENTY-ONE

FOREPLAY

DANTE...

A lessio sips his third Martini, narrowing his eyes as he studies my face. His long hair is plaited loosely behind him, a single strand of brown falling over his knitted brow as he waits for me to answer his question.

Sitting at the bar in one of his elegant Vegas clubs, close enough for our knees to touch, our "just one drink" had quickly turned to more as we caught each other up with our lives and feelings since our last rendezvous, a process that would never (and could never) be complete.

It took over six months for Alessio to return to his empire after the altercation with his brother that fateful Valentine's where Danica and I fled his club barefoot. As soon as he got back, that same weekend, he met us at the airport in a limo that I thought unnecessary but Danica loved.

Despite the initial awkward moments and difficult conversations, the three of us quickly found our rhythm, probably thanks to Danica more than anyone else. Picking the words had been a challenge, but I'd been working at it, one confession at a time.

But luckily my body didn't have that same hesitation when Alessio's was around. My body always knew it found a good match, even all those years ago. My body was as addicted to Alessio's as he was to mine. And Danica? Oh god, nobody could get enough of Danica.

I still wasn't sure what happened to Francesco. I knew he was still alive but got what he had coming to him. But I spared him little thought. There was no reason to think about any Santoro except the Dark Prince who was now the King.

And the King ensured we were treated like royalty every time we came to the city, which was way more often than planned. Turns out my wife-to-be was as taken with Alessio as she was with Vegas, and she thought up endless excuses to charter us back to the city that never sleeps. Not that I was complaining.

Sure, I should probably spend more time taking care of my actual work responsibilities, but saying no to Danica was harder than it seemed. The way her face lit up when she got what she desired always made me feel all fuzzy inside. Besides, Emilio had things under control at home.

So, no work for me this weekend. I'm free to focus on Alessio's knees against mine in this dimly lit club while I throw back another whiskey for courage.

Around us, the music thumps away in repetitive beats I would never choose for anything but a running playlist perhaps. Yet my heart somehow pounds even faster than the music every time I think about going back upstairs. *Tonight's the night...*

It's Valentine's Day again, but I don't pay attention to the decor, or the people. My view is filled with Alessio, my very own Lucifer Morningstar; the Devil himself with an empire of sinful vices. But the only sin I'm interested in tonight is Lust with a capital L.

As Alessio grins at me over that half-drunk Martini, he repeats his question, the one he always asks whenever he sees me. "Tell me, Don Fera, are you going to run away again?"

My answer is always the same. "I always come back, don't I?" I say, reaching for his hand. *Fuck who sees.* I don't care anymore.

"You almost didn't. I would've lost you forever if Danica didn't bring you to me last Valentine's." Alessio twirls his fingers around mine like they're dancing, twisting my new engagement ring that isn't that new anymore.

"Remind me to thank her again later," I reply, smiling as my mind drifts to my Queen just for a second. It's only been two hours since I last saw her, but I miss her already.

"We both can." Alessio guides my hand to his thigh, resting it there. His cock is mere inches away and I know it's hard, just like mine; its outline stands out beneath his tight pants.

He expects me to jerk my hand away, I know he does, but I don't. Instead, I squeeze his leg, my eyes retracing their path back to his, holding him captive.

"I worry about you, Alessio."

"Hmm, I like this. Emotion is a good look on that beautiful face. Something else I should thank Danica for?" Alessio jokes, moving my hand closer to his belt, onto his lap. His cock jumps under my touch, the fabric of his pants offering little interference.

As our game of chicken quickly gathers momentum, Alessio boldly stares me down, watching intently to see what I will do, right here, out in the open.

The place is pumping, packed with people; so many pairs of eyes that are sure to be watching the two six-foot-plus men flirting at the bar. And not just any two giant men, two Dons from enemy families. But as Danica would say: see who gives a fuck. Certainly not me.

Defiantly, I meet Alessio's gaze, smirking as I pull his face towards me with my hand behind his neck. In a single smooth move, my tongue is between his lips, forcing them open to let me in. Losing myself in the moment, I kiss him passionately, hungrily; like I can never get enough—because I can't.

I don't give a fuck who is there, who sees me groping and caressing the infamous Don Santoro, kissing him until the world falls away in the distance, a mere buzz in the background. The only person whose opinion I care about is Danica and she's given me full permission to do whatever I want with (and to) Alessio.

"My, my," Alessio pants, straightening out his shirt as he tries to steady his racing breath. "I'll be damned. Dante Fera has some balls after all."

I grin but catch myself before shrugging. "What can I say? I want you now and I wanted you then," I confess, no longer ashamed of the words.

"Hmm, I like the sound of that. Come on, enough foreplay, darling. The things I want to do to your body..." Alessio takes my willing hand and leads me to the glass elevator in the corner.

The doors aren't even fully closed when the nefarious monarch with the plaited hair grabs me like he's about to beat me up, pushing me against a cold glass wall of the elevator. Hands all over me, over my cock, Alessio kisses me fervently as we ascend to the top in full view of the dancing bodies below.

Too soon, the elevator spits us out into a stunning room with an incredible view, just like every other penthouse in the Santoro books I've seen over the past three months. Alessio liked to move around, "for safety reasons," he said.

Danica greets us by the elevator, amidst a sea of new shopping bags strewn around Alessio's suite chaotically. Earlier, she sent us downstairs for a drink so she could "shower and settle in" as she calls it, which usually just meant she needed to shave. But judging from the loot, she fit in some shopping too while we were away.

We all knew the real reason Danica sent me downstairs was to have some alone time with Alessio; to calm my nerves. Only one part of that plan worked though, and it wasn't the part that was supposed to make me feel less nervous.

While I struggle to regain my breath after our elevator make-out session, Alessio greets Danica with an elaborate kiss, lifting her onto her tippy toes.

Afterward, he peeks into her shopping bags with an interest I could never fake. "What did you buy, *bella mia*?"

"Toys and secrets!" she exclaims, and they giggle together.

"Hey, baby," she beckons me over, and I sweep her into my arms, spinning her around for my kiss.

"*Tesoro*," I whisper, holding her close.

"I see Alessio's got you hard again. Of course." Danica rolls her eyes playfully, running her hand over the bulge in my pants.

"Standard." This time, I shrug, much to Danica's delight. Her ridiculous vocabulary is rubbing off on me; I should watch myself.

"Well, good thing I bought this then..." She pulls a new pegging harness from an unbranded bag and, shortly after, the thickest dildo she has ever brought home—a bright blue one.

Alessio snatches it from her before I can get a decent look. "I like this. It's almost as big as me."

"Exactly what I thought. I can warm him up for you," Danica grins, and I grab the dildo from Alessio.

"I'm right here, you two. Don't I get a say about what goes in my ass?" I protest like we haven't planned out the entire night already. The new dildo is a nice touch; I'm glad Danica thought of it. It could be ours to use with

Alessio...The thought makes my cheeks flush, and I look away quickly.

Alessio rests his arm casually on Danica's shoulder, and they look at me with a twinkle of laughter.

"Fine, baby. What do *you* want in your ass?" Danica asks, amused.

I don't have to hesitate; I know what I want. "Both of you, obviously."

"So, plan A then?" Danica steals the dildo back.

"You go get dressed, *cara mia*. I'll get him ready for you," Alessio tells her, pulling me over for a kiss.

"Am I a toy now?" I complain with mock seriousness, unbuttoning Alessio's shirt as he tugs at my pants. Instantly, the urgency from the elevator returns, the fire.

"You will be once I finally bury my cock in your ass," Alessio whispers in my ear, nibbling on my ticklish lobe.

I gasp. The mere thought makes my cock twitch, especially with Alessio's hands all over it, pulling it free from my underwear.

We've spoken about it so many times, but today is the day I finally find out how it feels to have Alessio inside me. The three of us have played together in so many varying positions and roles over the past three months, but I've been hesitant to take him—and not just because of his sheer size.

Even through all my kinky parties and explorations, I've never had anyone in my ass but Danica. Being okay with that level of vulnerability is tough for a man like me. But I'm not scared anymore. I want this more than I'm afraid of it.

When Danica returns—a Goddess in heels and harness, her freshly-washed blue cock in hand, spreading lube from base to tip—Alessio and I are both already naked, playfully wrestling on the bed, giving each other nipple burns. I can't speak for the other Don, but I'm painfully hard.

"Are you ready, my love?" Danica asks, that dreamy look on her face—the one she gets when she watches Alessio and I together—and I nod.

She kisses my hair before guiding me into position. Like a good boy, I kneel on all fours at the edge of the bed, my feet hanging off the side. Despite feeling very exposed with my ass in the air like that, I'm reassured by the fact that I'm in the safest space possible—with Danica.

Alessio moves up to lie down beside me, perfectly angling himself so he can stroke both our cocks at the same time. Instantly, without reserve, I groan as his fingers play over my length, setting it on fire with his delicate touch.

Holding onto a pillow, I bite down on the soft material as Danica spreads me open, lubes me up, and fills me to the brim—first with her fingers, then with her new cock.

There is nothing on my mind but the nerve endings in my ass, the incredible fullness that feels too much, like I can't take anymore...but then I do. I take it all, focusing on the sensation of Alessio's hand on my erection to distract from the initial pain in my ass that quickly blooms to pleasure.

Whispering sweet, dirty nothings into my ear, Danica plays gently at first, getting me used to her incredible girth.

"Hold on, baby," she tells me, and I know I'm about to be fucked senseless.

I close my eyes as Danica plows into me repeatedly in a rhythm that has me begging for release almost instantly. It's hard to concentrate; my circuits are flooding with too many stimuli.

But it's not time yet, not like this.

"Suit up; he's almost ready," I hear Danica tell Alessio, and I lament the loss of his touch on my dick as he gets up. At the same time, the mere thought of what's coming next is enough to almost send me over the edge.

Danica tells Alessio to put on a condom, and then she suddenly pulls out so fast that I collapse onto the pillow.

"All warmed up. Such a pretty bum." She smacks my ass playfully before falling into Alessio's ready arms. He kisses her deeply as she spreads her fingers around his wrapped dick, whispering something only meant for their ears while stroking him to total hardness.

"Don't hurt him," she says, loud enough for me to hear, and then she's off. I don't know where Danica goes, but she doesn't stay and watch, not this time.

It's just Alessio and I.

CHAPTER TWENTY-TWO

FILLED

DANTE...

"She's right; you do have a pretty bum," Alessio teases, running his large hands over my ass, jolting my neglected cock into further desperation.

Aching to be filled again, I feel empty without Danica. But Alessio is in no rush to tag in; he takes his sweet time, tormenting me with little caresses and ticklish kisses.

The anticipation drives me wild!

I melt into the pillow as Alessio rubs his erection against my ass cheeks, the space between them, teasing me with the delectable friction.

"Can you take it all?" Alessio asks as he presses the tip of his head against my entrance in a move that completely erases my memory file for breathing. His cock feels big, too big to fit, but I know he's the perfect size.

"I want you inside," I growl the words Danica bemoans me so often. They sound good, sound right. And they're true: I really *do* want it, despite the pain and the discomfort I feel as my first love stretches me around his thickness, dousing his cock in more cold lube as he goes.

"Careful what you wish for, *amore mio*." He always says that, but thus far, I've never regretted having my wishes granted.

When he's pushed his girthy hardness entirely inside me, Alessio reaches around to my cock again, stroking it, distracting me from the size of him pressed against my insides.

"Fuck me," I hiss, arching my hips to thrust my cock into his hand, desperate for his touch.

"Fuck me, *who*?" Alessio demands, raising his voice as he pushes even deeper into me, stealing the air right from my lungs. "Say it!"

"Fuck me, Don Santoro...please," I mutter, holding onto the bedsheets with all my might as the lover I thought I could never have gives me what I thought I would never experience.

But he doesn't finish me off, not yet. I'm lost in a blur of passion when Alessio suddenly pulls out and demands that I turn around. *Cazzo!*

I groan bitterly but do as I'm told, flipping onto my back to face those playful amber eyes. There is no penthouse around us, there is no bed, there is just Alessio and I. My body is his for the taking—on loan with permission from my Owner.

"Bum up." Alessio slips a pillow underneath my ass and pushes my legs onto my chest, hooking them onto his shoulders so my ankles are resting on either side of his head. He moves my limbs around without effort, clearly as fit as he looks.

There is something so arousing about our equally matched strength. I've never had anyone handle my body like that; the women in my life were always way shorter than me. But it's different with Alessio; he throws me around like I'm small...and I let him.

"Don't clench, darling. Let me in." Eyes locked in an all-consuming gaze, Alessio finds my lubed hole again, thrusting his cock back inside with little of the gentleness he spared before. This time, I can see his face, see the wanting etched on his sweaty brow as he finally makes good on his 25-year-old promise to fuck me the way I deserve.

A howl rips through me as Alessio pushes inside me again and again, rougher each time. I have no pillow to hold onto this time, only Alessio's hips. My nails dig into his skin as I struggle to keep my faculties intact.

"Oh, *Dio mio!*" I exclaim as Alessio spreads his fingers over my cock that's dangerously close to dripping. It feels so incredible! Not just the physical sensation of having something smashing against my sensitive prostrate repeatedly, or the long fingers milking my cock, no, the body those extremities are attached to is making all the difference.

"God won't save you, *amore mio*. You're the Devil's plaything now," Alessio tells me, and something in me ignites, burning through my skin.

Unreserved and loud, we both moan in unison, and the sound of Alessio's pleasure sets me off, instantly driving me feral. The look on his face is the most mesmerizing thing; he looks so beautiful with that handsome face contorted in pleasure.

The groans, the gasps, the hurried breaths...they're warm on my neck, fueling my frenzy, as my cock leaks pre-cum onto Alessio's fingers. All I smell is Aramis, Aramis and lust.

Remembering to breathe is a challenge. My cock is ready to explode at any second. *Where's Danica?* I need permission.

As if almost on cue, the Mistress of my house waltzes into the room, towel in hand, drying off her freshly washed silicone cock.

"Care if I join you?" Danica grins, leaning down to kiss Alessio's neck. She looks through the gap under his arm, blowing me a kiss. "Hey, you." All I have to offer in return is a weak smile.

"I thought you'd never ask," Alessio answers with a grin, not hesitating for a second to accept the offer. It was the scene we planned, after all.

With his cock still buried deep inside me, our bodies fused into one, Alessio scoots me up, repositioning me on the bed to make space for him. As he joins me on the mattress, knees bent on the bed, he pushes my legs down onto my chest like we're doing some weird hamstring stretch, trapping my cock between our abs.

"Deep breaths, dear," Danica instructs, and I brace myself as well, eyes glued on Alessio's expression, the twitching of the little lines on his forehead as he concentrates.

"I'm ready," Alessio tells her, wincing as she spreads her lubed fingers inside, stretching him, prepping him. Soon, he's moaning in deep, low tones as Danica fingers his ass.

Beneath him, I lie completely still, overly aware of the fullness still inside me, the pre-cum smearing over both our stomachs as I try to keep my dick from exploding and ruining the moment...It's so damn hard though.

Alessio kisses me sweetly and then closes his eyes, pain rippling across his face momentarily as Danica's lubed cock follows the path of her fingers inside. Thrusting from behind, heeled feet still firmly on the floor, Danica's movement pushes Alessio deeper into me as well, and a loud groan creeps up my throat.

Danica smiles down at me, looking proud. "I love you, baby," she tells me, her blue cock buried fully in Alessio's ass, and I repeat the words between rapid breaths. My Queen reaches for my hand, squeezing affectionately, before shifting her grip to Alessio's waist, lifting one of her legs onto the bed to get better leverage.

Slowly initially, and then increasingly faster, we rock together at Danica's chosen pace, Alessio sandwiched between us, his cock slamming into me with every thrust of Danica's. My legs ache under their weight in this impossible position, but I spare almost no thought to the plight of my limbs—the pleasure overrides every other feeling.

When I can keep them open, my eyes dart from Alessio to Danica, and I can't help smiling like a fool. Being able to share Alessio with her is so special.

But I know I can't last much longer. My orgasm is building, building to a state of delirium under the glorious sweaty bodies grinding above me.

"Fuck," I growl in a husky tone like I'm auditioning for *The Witcher*, and I know my climax is near.

Danica knows that sound, knows what that desperation on my face means, and I'm grateful she chooses mercy rather than torment. Plunging into Alessio again, she whispers the words that set me free: "Come for me, baby."

But I'm not the one who explodes. Stimulated from both sides, Alessio comes first, collapsing on my chest in exhaustion. I'm only seconds behind, my groans echoing his as thick cum releases between us.

Danica pulls out immediately, de-skewering Alessio, and joining us on the bed. She hasn't had her orgasm, not this time, but she has two Dons at her service who'll make damn sure she does (again and again) before the night is over.

Alessio rolls off me with a loud grunt, and my freed legs find their feeling again, pestering me with their dull ache as I stretch them out. It's a small price to pay for the endorphins flooding my circuits

For a while, the three of us lie there on the bed, entangled in each other's sticky, sweaty bodies with rapid breaths echoing rapid heartbeats. *Is this what pure bliss feels like?*

Twenty-five years ago, I never thought I'd have this—Alessio's warmth against my left side, Danica curled into my right, both of them mine in different but equally precious ways.

There are no words in my mind, only overwhelming feelings that warm my belly and my cock in equal measure. Contentment, that's what this is. Peace. The kind I never thought someone like me deserved.

Alessio is the first to speak, which is no surprise. "I got your Christmas card, by the way. Cute dog," he says with a grin. Not exactly the expected declaration after our intimate threesome, but that's Alessio for you, a Joker at any age. Some things never change, thank god.

"You're deranged." I smile, shaking my head at him. His unpredictable mind is a mystery to me, but it couldn't be any other way. It's part of why I fell in love with him all those years ago, part of why I never stopped.

"And you, Don Fera—as always—are hard," Alessio retorts, lazily grabbing at my dick. His touch still sends electricity through my body, just like it did when we were young and stupid and thought love could conquer anything.

Danica laughs heartily. "It is a cute dog. You should come to visit us sometime," she offers, playing with Alessio's free hand in hers. The sight of them together—my past and my present, my two great loves —makes my chest tight with emotion.

"Hmm, I prefer to remain your Vegas-boy, if that's okay. I've got an empire to run this side." We share a knowing smile. Some boundaries are healthy, even in whatever this beautiful, unconventional thing between us has become.

"Will you come to the wedding at least?" Danica asks, somewhat disappointed.

Alessio looks at me, one eyebrow raised in question. "If you invite me." There's something vulnerable in his eyes, a echo of old wounds we're still healing.

"Woah, slow down you two. It's still early days. We need to plan the whole thing still." I laugh, pulling them both closer to me. My Queen and my Vegas King, both perfectly imperfect for me in their own ways.

"Can you imagine the scandal of having the one and only Don Santoro at our wedding?" Danica giggles, eyes bright with excitement. She's already planning mischief—I can see it in her smile.

"That sounds like fun." Alessio winks at me. "Perhaps it's time our families finally bury the hatchet?"

I grab his face for a messy kiss. "It's time."

As we drift toward sleep, our breathing synchronizes, three heartbeats finding their own rhythm together. Danica's fingers trace lazy patterns on my chest while Alessio's arm drapes possessively across us both. The neon lights of Vegas paint shadows through the window, but for once, they don't feel like warnings.

They say Dons don't get happy endings. We're too steeped in blood, too weighted by power, too scarred by the lives we've chosen. But maybe that's because we look for happiness in the wrong places—in control instead of surrender, in power instead of love, in tradition instead of truth.

I press a kiss to Danica's temple, then turn to catch Alessio's knowing smile. My Queen and my first love, both mine in different ways, both teaching me that strength comes in many forms. That sometimes the bravest thing a Don can do is kneel.

Tomorrow, we'll return to our separate kingdoms—Alessio to his glittering empire, Danica and I to our world of shadows. But something has shifted, realigned. The walls between our worlds have crumbled, leaving something better in their place.

Something that tastes like freedom.

Something that feels like home.

Something worth waiting twenty-five years to find.

Oh, Dio mio. What is this life?

###

This is not the end for these three. Danica and her two Dons will return in Madame Danica, Book 4. To find out more, check out mkaynoir.com/madame

THANK YOU

Thank you for reading my book.

If you enjoyed it, wouldn't you please take a moment to leave me a **review** at your favorite retailer? It helps more like-minded people to find this very niche content.

Do you want more stories with this vibe? Then carry on reading...

To get bonus content and fresh releases, join my **newsletter** or follow me on **BookBub**.

Kay

MORE BY M KAY NOIR

Madame Danica

Queens & Knights Book 4

***

The explosive final book in the Queens & Knights series brings danger, devotion, and delicious darkness. This conclusion of Dante and Danica's spicy love story features morally grey characters, graphic violence, polyamory, and strong power exchange themes (see my website for the full TW list). Reading the series in order is recommended. HEA guaranteed.

ABOUT THE AUTHOR

M Kay Noir is a queer romance author and journalist obsessed with moments of desire. Most of her stories are kinky, queer-friendly, polyamorous undertakings with neurotic characters who are often their own worst enemy. If you expect any regard for traditional gender roles or power dynamics, you will be disappointed.

Kay has been penning steamy moments for more than 15 years now, from fanfics to ghostwriting and now finally her own stories. Her day job also involves a lot of writing, albeit a different kind—mostly sustainability things. When she's not writing (or reading), she enjoys making her husband look at yet another sunset and watching live music concerts.

**See mkaynoir.com for the long version.